THE
LONE
RANGER

Adapted by Elizabeth Rudnick

Based on the screenplay by Justin Haythe and Ted Elliott & Terry Rossio
Screen Story by Ted Elliott & Terry Rossio and Justin Haythe
Produced by Jerry Bruckheimer, Gore Verbinski
Directed by Gore Verbinski

DISNEY PRESS
New York

Printed in the United States of America

First Edition

1 3 5 7 9 10 8 6 4 2

ISBN 978-1-4231-7715-9

For more Disney Press fun, visit disneybooks.com

For more Lone Ranger fun, visit www.disney.go.com/the-lone-ranger

SUSTAINABLE FORESTRY INITIATIVE

Certified Chain of Custody
Promoting Sustainable Forestry

www.sfiprogram.org

SFI-01054

The SFI label applies to the text stock

PROLOGUE

San Francisco, July 1933. In the bustling City by the Bay, it was hard to tell that the rest of the country was in the midst of one of the worst years of its young history. Instead of dust bowls and depression, San Francisco was booming. Steamships dotted the harbor, while up on the hill, cranes lifted beams high into the skyline.

Amid all of it, a fairground had been set up, its bright lights warm and welcoming against the dimming sky. Families wandered the fair, children in tow, while young men attempted to impress their girlfriends with cotton candy and big stuffed animals. Amid it all, a carousel circled slowly, giving its passengers time to take in the San Francisco skyline and the tiny people below.

A young boy with a toy six-shooter strapped to his hip strode through the fair, a bemused look on his face. His name was Will, and he had seen it all before. The games, the shows, the silly carousel that was far too slow for the likes of him. There was only one thing that interested him about the fairground—the Wild West Show. It was supposed to be the "greatest show on Earth." But Will wanted to see for himself. Reaching up, he adjusted the mask he wore over his eyes and ducked inside the tent.

As his eyes adjusted to the gloom, Will made out several dioramas depicting scenes from the Wild West. There was a stuffed bison next to a big stuffed bear, both of their coats missing fur in spots. Nearby, a covered wagon was frozen in motion, its white canopy aged and yellowed. Walking along, Will sighed. Everything looked old and fake. He wanted to see something exciting. Something . . . real.

He came to a stop in front of one of the dioramas. The sign above read THE NOBLE SAVAGE IN HIS NATURAL HABITAT. Inside sat a lifeless Comanche Indian, his ancient face covered in white and black paint. On his head perched a stuffed crow with faded black feathers. As the rest of the crowd moved along to the next diorama, Will stayed back, absently eating from his bag of peanuts. He had never seen a real Comanche Indian. Even though he knew it was just a statue, he couldn't help leaning in closer.

Suddenly, the Comanche Indian's eyes flickered.

With a gasp, Will dropped his bag of peanuts and took a step back. Reaching down, he pulled out his toy gun and fired. The harmless caps sounded loud, but the sound of Will's pounding heart was even louder.

"Kemosabe?" the old Comanche Indian said, his voice scratchy. He leaned forward, narrowing his ancient, watery eyes. "You bring horses?"

"I think you made a mistake, mister," Will said hesitantly.

A sadness seemed to settle over the old man as he looked down at Will. The intense gaze made Will nervous and he took a step back, stepping on a peanut shell. The crack startled him anew and his heart began to race again.

Looking at the bag of peanuts that had fallen to the floor, the Comanche raised an eyebrow. "Make trade?" he asked.

Will glanced down at the peanuts and then back at the Comanche. With a shrug, he retrieved the snack and tentatively handed it over. The elderly man took the bag from Will's palm, replacing it with the corpse of a mummified mouse. Will recoiled in disgust. Then, gulping, he nodded his thanks.

As the Comanche munched on a peanut, Will lowered his mask to try to get a closer look. He knew that he wasn't imagining it. The Comanche Indian was most definitely alive. But how? And why had he chosen to speak to him of all people?

"Never take off the mask," the man said, breaking into Will's thoughts.

"Why not?" Will asked.

The old Comanche closed his eyes as a long-forgotten memory surfaced. He began to speak, so softly Will had to strain to hear his story. . . .

On a hilltop, hidden among the trees, the Comanche Indian, now clearly much younger, sat astride his horse, gazing into the horizon, the same stuffed crow perched on his head. Next to him, on a horse of his own, sat a man who wore a white hat and a black mask.

As they sat there, the man adjusted his mask, clearly uncomfortable. "You sure about this?" he asked.

The Comanche looked at him, then returned his gaze to the horizon before speaking. "Dead man strike fear into the heart of his enemies," he said cryptically.

"All right," the man replied with a sigh. "Let's do this."

Kicking their horses' sides, the two men burst out of their cover and thundered down the hill. Within moments, they had reached a small town nestled into the hillside. Wooden buildings lined the one main street, and as they raced through, people scattered out of the way. The masked man and the Comanche Indian reined their horses to a stop in front of one of the larger buildings—the Colby Municipal Bank.

Jumping off their horses, the men burst through the doors. "Ladies and gentlemen," the masked man announced, "my colleague and I will be making a withdrawal. . . ."

For a moment nobody said a thing. Then a man wearing a stovepipe hat took a step forward. "What are you two supposed to be?" he asked, sounding more confused than scared.

The masked man exchanged glances with his compatriot. "I told you," he said under his breath. "I feel ridiculous. Maybe if we go out and come in again . . ."

Before he could finish his thought, the Comanche Indian whipped out his tomahawk and threw it across the room. It sliced the man's hat in two before thudding into the clock on the wall behind him. Taking the cue, the masked man pulled out his gun and fired into the air. A huge chandelier crashed to the ground, shattering and causing the customers to scream.

"Guess I didn't make myself clear," the masked man said. "This is a bank robbery!"

Together, he and the Comanche Indian leaped over the counter and made their way toward the safe. . . .

Will had been listening wide-eyed to the old man's story. But now he stopped him. "Wait a minute," he said, realization dawning. He knew who the Comanche was! And the masked man! He had read all about them in his adventure stories. "You're saying you're Tonto? *The* Tonto?"

"There is another?" the old man asked.

"But . . . the Lone Ranger and Tonto were good guys!" Will protested. "I mean, they didn't rob banks—did they?"

For a moment, Tonto was silent. Then he spoke, his voice stronger and full of the wisdom of many years. "There comes a time," he said, "when a good man must wear a mask. . . ."

CHAPTER 1

Colby, Texas, 1869

The air was dusty and full of the sounds of men hard at work. Hammers clanged against steel as men of every race and creed laid down hundred-pound railroad ties. Dirt billowed into the already thick air as other men hacked away, creating trenches out of the hard desert floor. Parked nearby, waiting to move forward, was the great and mighty Constitution—one of the biggest and fastest locomotives ever built.

In the midst of all the work, a man stood before a small crowd. Unlike the workers behind him, Latham Cole was impeccably dressed. He carried himself like the war hero and railroad man he was, his shoulders high and his chin higher still. Next to him, Sheriff Garrick P. Donovan stood, scanning the crowd to ensure no one caused any trouble. Cole had been clear. This was a very important day.

Clearing his throat, Cole stepped forward. "Ladies and gentlemen," he began, "I have asked you here today to see firsthand what I believe to be the single greatest enterprise under God." He paused and gestured to the tracks being laid behind him. "To unite this great country by iron rail."

The crowd let out a round of applause and Cole soaked it in, loving the attention that *his* tracks, and *he*, were getting. His eyes drifted to one audience member in particular. Standing toward the back, her hands still, was Rebecca Reid. Even in her worn work clothes and dust-stained boots, she was beautiful, and Cole found himself losing focus. Shaking his head, he continued.

"Our crews are laying track at an unprecedented rate of ten miles a day, and God willing, we will reach Promontory Summit by summer's end." Once again, the crowd erupted in applause. Cole turned his attention toward a group of Comanche Indians standing together at the edge of the crowd. One of the men, Red Knee, returned Cole's stare with his one eye, the other lost in battle years before. "To the Comanche," Cole went on, "I say, you have nothing to fear. I fought four years with the army of Ulysses S. Grant and I too am tired of war. As long as there is peace between us, all land treaties will be honored."

Red Knee's face remained emotionless, the words falling on deaf ears. Turning, he walked away, the rest of his men following close behind.

Cole ignored the snub. He hadn't expected anything different. After all, the war between them had been going on for a long time. Even now, despite the treaties and the peace offerings, things were tense, especially out here in the frontier. And not just because of the Comanche. Cole began to speak once more. "To the outlaws—those who prey on the weak—I say, make no mistake. Law and order has come to the Wild West. . . ."

On cue, Sheriff Donovan unrolled a large piece of paper and held it up. On the front were the all-too-familiar word WANTED and, beneath, the picture of an outlaw, his face burned on one side.

"That is why I am bringing the notorious outlaw and Indian killer Butch Cavendish here to hang for his crimes," Cole said, gesturing at the poster. "The future is bright, ladies and gentlemen. And it's just around the bend."

As the crowd erupted into whistles and cheers, Cole waved and smiled. When the crowd had finally dispersed, he made his way toward a makeshift market that had been set up on the street. His speech had gone perfectly. The people loved him, and when he brought Cavendish to justice, they would love him even more. Nothing could mar his good mood.

"Afternoon, Latham," a voice cooed in his ear, interrupting his thoughts. As he turned, the smile disappeared from his lips. Standing in front of him was a woman with shockingly red hair, a tiny waist, and a bright and flashy dress. Red Harrington. It made Cole uncomfortable just to be seen talking to such an improper lady. But she clearly didn't care. "Just wanted to let you know how grateful I am for the chance to see that animal hang," the woman went on.

"Indeed. Now, if you'll excuse me, Miss Harrington, I have business to see to," Cole said dismissively as he began to push past her.

Red Harrington raised one perfectly arched eyebrow. "Still having train trouble?" she asked his retreating back. Cole stopped and turned. With a wink, she spun on her heel and walked away, a barely noticeable limp to her step.

Stifling a groan, Cole continued through the market. Every other step or so, someone would come up to shake his hand or say congratulations, slowing his progress. But eventually, he found what—or rather who—he was looking for.

Rebecca Reid stood in front of a table covered in silk scarves and bright folded parasols. A newspaper ad was on display, showing beautiful women wearing the scarves in a bustling city, the epitome of high fashion. Rebecca's seven-year-old son, Danny, stood beside her, using his finger as a pretend gun to shoot at the items in the various stalls.

Picking up a stunning blue scarf, Rebecca held it to her chest, admiring the soft texture and vivid color. Kai, a small Chinese woman who worked at the stall, smiled and held up a mirror. Gazing at her reflection, Rebecca smiled. For a moment, she actually felt . . . beautiful.

Suddenly, Kai put down the mirror. "For you," she said, forcing the scarf into Rebecca's hand. Confused, Rebecca tried to protest, but another voice stopped her. Turning, she found herself face-to-face with Latham Cole.

"She's right," he said. "Matches your eyes."

Embarrassed by the attention, Rebecca nodded her thanks to Kai and then stuffed the scarf deep into her pocket. Together, she and Cole walked on, Danny following close behind.

"I didn't think you'd make it out, Mrs. Reid," Cole said after a moment of silence.

Rebecca shrugged. "Just wanted to see what all the fuss was about," she answered matter-of-factly. She felt Cole's shoulder brush hers and stifled a shudder. She was a married woman. Yet he was always seeking out her attention. It was unnerving.

"And what do you think of our endeavor?" Cole went on, apparently oblivious.

"Looks to me like a lot of men digging in the desert," she replied.

Cole didn't reply. Instead, he turned to Danny. "Ever had a bluepoint oyster?" The young boy shook his head. "One day soon, you'll be able to get on a train right here in Colby, ride it all the way to San Francisco, eating New York oysters packed in ice. Sail on to China and come back around the other side if you want to."

"That true, Mama?" Danny asked, his eyes wide.

"I'll believe it when I see it," Rebecca replied warily.

They had come to a stop in front of a stall with various children's toys displayed. Picking up one of them, Cole twirled it in his hand. Dropping a coin on the table, he handed the toy to Danny, who eagerly grabbed it. "I expect on a lawman's salary, a lot must fall on you," Cole said, looking at Rebecca.

Taking the toy out of Danny's hand, she placed it back on the table. "We do just fine, thank you," she replied icily. True, being on the farm all by herself while her husband and his men roamed the wilds wasn't easy, but it did no good to dwell on it. It was her life—hardship and all. And it was the sacrifice she had made when she married Dan Reid, Texas Ranger.

Cole seemed to sense that he had pushed Rebecca hard enough. "I meant no disrespect," he said, holding his hands up apologetically. "They don't make men like your husband anymore. Kind that settled this country. Fact is, I envy him:

a fine family, a boy to carry his name." He paused, his eyes lingering on Rebecca for a moment too long. "I just hate to see a bird in a cage."

Tipping his hat, Cole turned and walked away. Behind him, Rebecca watched him go, her eyes narrowed. The man gave her the willies.

✪ ✪ ✪

At that moment, Dan Reid was standing on a train platform in another town in another part of the same godforsaken desert. Beside him, five other men in long, dusty jackets, their hats pulled low over their eyes, spread out along the platform, causing people to scuttle away nervously. Walking over to the telegraph operator, Dan pulled his jacket aside, revealing the bright silver badge that marked him as a ranger.

The telegraph operator eyed the badge, then looked down at the message he had just received. The name Cavendish was bold on the page. The deadly outlaw's name was infamous throughout the West. "Run a man all the way to the state line, put him on a train, and ship him right back," the operator said. "Don't make no sense."

Clayton, another one of the rangers, stepped up and dipped his hand into the candy jar on the operator's desk. "Guess they run out of hanging rope in Oklahoma," he said, unwrapping the candy.

"Mr. Cole wants to make an example," said Navarro, a handsome ranger with dark hair and thick eyebrows, as he gazed at his reflection in the window.

"Word is, Cavendish is looking for payback with you, Dan," said a ranger by the name of Martin. Next to him, Ranger Blaine nodded.

"They say he ate a red-legger's heart in the Missouri wars," Blaine said, eager to add his two cents. "Swallowed it whole, still beating the man's blood."

"Heard it was the eyes, and he used a toothpick like a pair of pickled onions," Martin added.

Navarro shook his head.

"Which is it, Dan?" Martin asked, turning to the head ranger.

Squinting into the distance, Reid shrugged his wide shoulders, causing dust to fall off his jacket. "Don't see how it makes a difference," he said.

Dan Reid didn't have time to listen to stories or argue over the outlaw's rumored kills. The outlaw himself was heading their way on a speeding train. And when that train arrived, it would be up to Dan and his men to get Cavendish safely to Colby. If they didn't, the stories wouldn't matter, because the outlaw would be on the loose once more, free to make plenty of new ones.

CHAPTER 2

John Reid sat, lost in thought, as the train he was riding on brought him closer and closer to his destination. Farther up in the car, a preacher led a group of women in prayer. But John hardly noticed. It had been eight years since he had been back to Colby. Nine years since he had left the comfort and safety of his home and family to go to college. When he had left, he had been an uneducated boy, rough around the edges. Now he was coming back a lawyer, complete with a new three-piece suit. Yet instead of being excited, he felt his stomach flutter and he nervously opened the book on his lap and took out a photograph. Its edges were rough with wear, but the photo was still clear. In it, Rebecca posed on a wooden chair beside a riverbank. Gently, John reached out and traced her face, a motion he had made countless times before.

Suddenly, a doll landed at John's feet. Startled, he raised his eyes and saw a young girl sitting across the aisle, eyeing the doll plaintively. Reaching down, John picked up the doll and smoothed her dress. He smiled and then tossed it across the aisle. But no sooner had the doll left his hands than a gust of wind from an open window rushed through the train car. As John and the young girl watched in horror, the doll was pulled right out another window.

There was a moment of silence and then the girl began to cry. Loudly.

The cries caused her mother, who had been praying along with the preacher, to stop and turn to John. Noticing his concern, she smiled. "Care to pray with us?" she asked.

John returned the smile but shook his head. "Much obliged, but this here is my bible," he said, holding up his most prized possession—a copy of John Locke's *Two Treatises of Government.*

As the woman returned to her prayer, John noticed a large, rough-looking man with a big mustache making his way down the aisle of the train car. John shifted in his seat, nervous, until he noticed the bright silver badge on the man's belt. He was a Texas Ranger. Smiling, John relaxed back in his seat as the ranger continued past him and made his way out the back of the car.

As the wind whistled by, the ranger straddled the gap between the two cars. Beneath him, metal flashed as the train rushed over the tracks. He reached out and knocked on the door in front of him. There was the sound of a bolt sliding and then the door swung open.

Inside, the car was empty save for three people—another ranger and two prisoners. The mustached ranger made his way over and handed his partner a cold drink. Then he turned and kicked the chained leg of one of the prisoners. "Almost hanging time, Butch," he sneered. The prisoner didn't move. "Hear what I said, boy?"

Finally, the man looked up. The WANTED poster had not done Butch Cavendish justice. Not only was his face burned on one side, he had a multitude of long scars from being stabbed and round ones where he'd been shot. Still, he sat whistling as though he had not a care in the world.

Turning from Cavendish, the ranger eyed the other prisoner. It was Tonto. He sat chained to an eyelet in the floor. In his hand he held a broken pocket watch. As the ranger looked on, the Comanche Indian spun the watch into the air, caught it, and then tried to flick it open almost like a lighter. It didn't work. Frustrated, he started the move again.

"It's broke, Indian," the ranger said. "Can't you see that?"

He looked up, a blank expression on his painted face.

Frustrated by Cavendish's cheer and Tonto's apparent lack of understanding, the lawman sighed and took a seat next to his partner. Pulling out a deck of cards, they began to play. All they had to do was make sure the two chained prisoners stayed chained. How hard could that be?

❋ ❋ ❋

As the rangers played cards, Tonto chanted softly to himself, flipping the broken pocket watch over and over again. He was trying to get it to open in one move, like men did with their fancy metal lighters. Finally, he gave up. As he slipped the watch into his pouch, he noticed Cavendish fidgeting. Taking a closer look, Tonto saw that the other prisoner had worked his fingers bloody getting a nail loose from the wooden floorboard. Over Cavendish's shoulder, the rangers continued their game, unaware.

Tonto began to chant louder.

Slowly, Cavendish removed another nail from the floor.

Tonto chanted even louder.

Then Cavendish pulled up the floorboard completely.

Tonto chanted even louder as he watched Cavendish pull a pistol out from under the floorboard.

Looking up, the outlaw saw Tonto watching him. He raised a finger to his lips. Tonto stopped chanting.

"Bathroom break, boss?" Cavendish asked the unsuspecting rangers.

"Nerves, huh?" the mustached ranger said as he stood up and made his way over to the outlaw.

As the ranger accompanied Cavendish toward a foul-looking latrine in the corner of the train car, Tonto reached into his pouch and pulled out a handful of birdseed. He threw a little bit toward the ranger. Nothing. He threw a little more. Still nothing. Finally, he threw a lot. The lawman looked over and Tonto began gesturing wildly at Cavendish. Then he formed a gun with his pointer finger and thumb. The ranger's eyes grew wide as understanding dawned. He reached for his gun.

But it was too late.

At that moment, Cavendish turned, his own gun in hand. BOOM! With a single blast, he shot the mustached lawman. Then he fired at the other ranger, who fell to the floor with a thud. His gun smoking, Cavendish turned and eyed Tonto. He was still seated, his hand in the shape of a gun. As if he hadn't done a thing, Tonto reached into his pouch, pulled out more seed, and began to feed his bird.

John Reid stared out the window at the shadow of the train as it raced over the desert floor. For the past few hours, it had been the same shadow on the same dry, dusty ground. But suddenly, something looked different. The train's roof seemed to have changed shape. Squinting, John realized it was the shadow of a man. Someone was riding on the roof of the car!

Curious, John stood up and made his way toward the back of the car. As he pushed the door open, the wind whipped through his hair and knocked him backward. Struggling, he stepped outside and peered up the ladder that led to the train's roof. Just as he was about to step onto the ladder, he glanced through the small window of the next car. His foot hovered over the ladder as he made out a pair of legs. The legs weren't moving.

John grabbed the fire ax secured to the wall of the train car and raised it above his head. He didn't know what was going on, but he was determined to find out.

CHAPTER 3

Inside the prison car, Tonto found himself staring down the barrel of Cavendish's gun. As calmly as possible, the Comanche Indian continued to feed his bird.

"Fifteen hours I've watched you feed that bird," Cavendish said, his jaw clenched. "Gets on a man's nerves."

"Bird hungry," Tonto replied. "Birdy num-num."

Cavendish cocked his head, pressing the gun harder into Tonto's forehead. "You really are crazy, aren't you?"

Tonto stopped feeding the bird and leveled his gaze at the outlaw. "I do not fear what comes next," he replied.

Cocking his gun, Cavendish smiled cruelly. "Nothing comes next," he said as he began to pull back on the trigger.

CRASH!

Behind them, the door of the train car burst open, revealing John Reid. Spinning around, Cavendish aimed the gun at the man's face. He looked him up and down. "Nice suit," Cavendish sneered, once again preparing to fire. But before he could shoot, Cavendish heard the sound of another gun cocking—right behind him. Spinning around again, he saw Tonto holding the dead ranger's pistol, a wild, murderous look in his eye.

"Time has finally come, Windigo," Tonto said, the gun steady in his hand.

Windigo? The word echoed through Cavendish's mind, reminding him of something from long before. Slowly, the outlaw leaned down and put his gun on the floor. "I know you, Indian?" he asked.

Tonto held out his pocket watch. "You know me," he answered. "You know me by the screams of my ancestors in the desert wind, as you will know their cries of joy when I finally wipe you from the face of the earth." He tensed his finger on the trigger, ready to fire. . . .

THUNK!

In one swift move, John knocked the gun from Tonto's hand, kicked it away, and then swooped down to pick up Cavendish's. "That won't be necessary," John said. Letting out a cry of rage, Tonto lunged at John. But he was still chained and the heavy metal jolted him backward. "As district attorney," John went on, slapping a pair of manacles on the outlaw, "I'll see to it he's prosecuted to the full extent of the law."

"What kind of lawman don't carry his own gun?" Cavendish asked, straining against the manacles to no avail.

"Where this train's heading, there's no place for men who do," John replied.

Cavendish raised an eyebrow as Tonto hung his head. "Yeah, where's that?"

"The future," John said as he opened the gun and dumped the unused shells on the floor. Satisfied, he started to say more when the side door of the car slid open, revealing five men on horseback. Their guns turned on John. Cavendish's men had arrived.

In seconds, they had an unarmed John chained to the floor beside Tonto as Cavendish made his escape. Walking over to the side door, Cavendish paused and turned to look back at the two men. "Lawyer and a crazy Indian," he said, chuckling. "Bet you two got a lot to talk about." He looked out the door toward the front of the train. Thanks to his men, the engineer was no longer running the engine. The train was barreling along with no one in control. "Best make it quick," Cavendish added over his shoulder. Then, with another laugh, he leaped out, landing on his horse.

As the train raced along, gaining speed, John turned to

Tonto. The Comanche looked at him, hatred all over his face. John gulped. Perhaps he should have put a bit more thought into the plan. What was he going to do now?

✪ ✪ ✪

Ranger Dan Reid stood on the platform, watching as the train carrying his outlaw appeared on the horizon. He nodded, pleased to see that things were going according to schedule. But then he squinted. The train was going fast. Too fast.

As if reading his thoughts, the telegraph operator came and stood beside him. "Should be slowing down by now," the old man observed.

The men watched as the train came closer and closer, the whir of its wheels growing louder and louder. With a whoosh, the train sped by the platform, leaving only a billow of dust and the smell of coal behind.

Moments later, the rangers were on their horses and racing after the runaway train. But how were they ever going to catch up with the iron beast? And if they couldn't, what was going to happen to all the passengers?

✪ ✪ ✪

Inside the train car, John and Tonto sat in uncomfortable silence. Trying to think of something to say, John eyed the bird atop Tonto's head. "You know," he began, "I did a little bird-watching myself growing up. You've done a wonderful job there with, uh . . ." His voice trailed off as Tonto raised his eyes and glared at him. "Anyway . . . I'm sure we'll be in the station any minute."

As if on cue, the platform flashed by.

Now completely terrified, John began to pull at his chains, trying to loosen them. "Reinforced Bethlehem steel," he muttered to himself. "Any attempt at escape is futile."

While John panicked, Tonto calmly reached out his foot and hooked his toes around the ax John had dropped. He pulled the tool toward him until it was close enough to grab. Then, using the blade, he pried up the floorboard that his chain was attached to. With a heavy stamp of his foot, the board came loose. Tonto was free.

Looking up, John saw the now free Tonto and stopped struggling. "For coming to the aid of a federal prosecutor, I'll be sure to put in a good word with the judge," he said, trying to bargain.

Tonto said nothing. Instead, he dropped the ax and began to walk away. Slowly, the chain slid through the eyelet and then—SNAP—it caught! Looking back, Tonto narrowed his eyes. While he had successfully unhooked himself from the floor, he was, annoyingly, still attached to John.

For a moment, the two men just looked at each other. While neither one of them liked the idea, it was clear they weren't going anywhere alone. And they definitely could not stay put. Outside, the landscape was going by faster and faster as the train continued to pick up speed.

John racked his brain, trying to come up with a plan. But law school had not prepared him for this kind of situation. An indecisive jury? He could sway them. A stubborn judge? He could debate him. But a train with no engineer, full of innocent passengers? That was clearly beyond his scope.

Before he could do anything, Tonto tugged on the chain, yanking John to his feet. He began dragging him toward the door. Moments later, they were standing on top of the speeding train. In the distance, John could make out the end of the line. He gulped. What now?

"We jump," Tonto said, as if reading his thoughts.

The Comanche took a step forward, but John yanked him back. "The passengers," he said.

"They jump," Tonto replied with a shrug.

"There are children on board!" John protested. "Have you no decency?"

Suddenly, Tonto's face filled with fury and his eyes narrowed. "Windigo getting away!" he shouted. With a fierce tug, he pulled John closer to the edge. John pulled back. Tonto dug in his heels and heaved. Soon the two men were in the midst of a dangerous game of tug-of-war. With each pull, they moved closer and closer to the train's edge.

Just when it looked like they were both going to plummet to the ground, they heard a noise behind them. Turning, they saw Jesus, one of Cavendish's men, clambering onto the roof of the train car. Without saying a word, John and Tonto began to run right at the outlaw, the chain pulled taut between them. When they reached Jesus, the chain acted like a clothesline, hitting the outlaw right in the middle of his chest and knocking him off his feet.

John raised his hands in victory. But at that very moment, they passed under a big hook set up to take mail deliveries. John's chain caught on the hook, and with a cry, he went flying.

Tonto smiled, happy to have his ball and chain gone, literally. And then his own chain went taut and he found himself flying through the air after John. As he whipped over the car's roof, he snagged Jesus's legs and threw him through a window into the passenger car before landing with a thud several cars back. Shakily, Tonto got to his feet. John was already standing, his eyes trained on another one of Cavendish's men, Frank. The outlaw was holding a suitcase overflowing with what looked like women's clothes.

"Why don't you put that down and settle this like men?" John said, raising his fists. "Though I warn you, I boxed in law school."

THWACK!

Frank popped John in the nose with the butt of his gun.

"OW!" John cried.

As John cradled his face, he heard a whir. Looking up, he watched with wide eyes as a lariat flew through the air and snapped around Frank's leg. A moment later, the outlaw was yanked off the train. Wheeling around, John smiled.

Racing alongside the train was Dan Reid. As John watched, Dan dropped the lariat, and Frank, in the dust and then slowly stood up on the saddle of his galloping horse. Holding out his arms for balance, he wavered for only a moment before leaping onto the speeding train.

"Great warrior," Tonto said, watching.

"Yeah, that's my brother," John said, rubbing his nose as Dan clambered up the side of the train and began walking toward them.

"Nice suit," Dan said without even acknowledging the Comanche chained to his brother's side.

Ignoring the rub, John began to follow him. "We have to stop the train," he said.

"No time," Dan responded.

John raised an eyebrow. That didn't sound like his bigger-than-life hero ranger brother. He had to have a plan. "I'm not leaving the passengers," John insisted.

"So help me unhook the cars," Dan replied simply.

Sooner than John would have liked, he found himself

back outside the prison car. The only car in front of them was the engine. They needed to unhook the link-and-pin coupler that attached the engine to the passenger cars behind. But there was a problem. The link and pin wouldn't budge. They were jammed together, and no matter how hard Dan and John pulled at it, they couldn't get the pin free.

Tonto, who had been mostly silent as the two brothers worried at the pin, suddenly held the chain out to John. "Hold this," he said. Then, as John watched in horror, Tonto let himself fall backward under the train.

As John struggled to keep the chain taut and keep Tonto from hitting the ground, Dan continued to pull at the coupler holding the pin down. With a groan, he lifted it just enough for the pin to come clear. Seeing his chance, Tonto kicked out with his foot, knocking the pin completely free.

There was a jolt and then a loud groan as the engine began to ease away from the passenger cars. Quickly, John pulled Tonto to safety.

"John!"

Looking up at the sound of his brother's cry, John let out his own groan. Somehow, he and Tonto had ended up on the engine side of the platform. Now, as he watched in horror, they moved farther and farther from the safety of the passenger cars.

And up ahead, the track was at an end. . . .

CHAPTER 4

With an unholy scream, the engine went off the end of the track. As it flew through the air, it hit a stack of wooden ties, causing them to splinter and shatter like matchsticks. The engine hovered for a moment in midair before slamming into the ground, its nose pushing through the dirt.

The force of the impact sent John and Tonto flying through the air, end over end, as forty tons of spinning steel groaned and shrieked behind them. Suddenly, a sharp rod was ripped from the engine's side. It shot straight at the pair, slicing their chain in half. They flew apart, and a moment later, the train finally came to a stop.

As the dust cleared, Tonto slowly got to his feet. Looking

down, he saw the broken chain and smiled. That hadn't been so bad. He brushed himself off and began to walk away.

"Hold it right there," John said. Tonto turned around. John stood right behind him, his hands still chained, but a determined look on his face. "I'm afraid I have to take you in."

Tonto stared at him for a moment. Then he resumed walking.

"Did you hear what I just said?" John asked, grabbing Tonto.

In one swift, effortless move, Tonto flipped him over his shoulder and onto the ground. But John wasn't giving up. He reached out and wrapped his arms around the Comanche's leg. Shrugging, Tonto began dragging him through the dirt. He wasn't about to give up either.

"By the authority granted me," John said, coughing as dirt filled his mouth, "by the state of Texas, I'm arresting you."

Suddenly, Tonto stopped. Standing right in front of him was Dan Reid's horse.

"All right there, little brother?" Dan asked, trying to hide his amusement.

"I'm taking this man into custody," John said, looking up, his face covered with dirt.

Dan was quiet, his expression unreadable, as he eyed his brother and then Tonto. Finally, he spoke. "What do you say we give the Indian a head start, considering what he did for the passengers?"

Tonto nodded. That sounded like a good idea to him. At least one of the brothers seemed rational.

Getting to his feet, John shook his head. "He was on the train for a reason, Dan."

"Probably," Dan replied. He turned his attention back to Tonto. "What's your crime?"

Tonto shrugged. "Indian," he said.

"*And* a man in the eyes of the law," John added. "Now, throw me your cuffs." He held out his hand toward Dan. His brother didn't make a move. "Dan . . . your cuffs," John repeated.

Finally, Dan dropped the cuffs into the dirt. "Whatever you say, little brother." He turned and he began to ride away. His brother had a lot to learn now that he was back.

✪ ✪ ✪

Inside the Colby jailhouse, John shut a cell door with a clang. On the other side of the bars, Tonto glared at him—an expression he was growing all too used to. But John was a man of the law. And while his brother seemed to think that the law could be flexible, he knew there was just the right way and the wrong way. He wasn't going to feel bad for doing the right thing.

"Dan?"

The sound of a woman's voice—a familiar woman's voice—made John turn. Standing there was Rebecca, her beautiful face both the same and so different from the last time he had seen it, many years before.

Realizing he was not her husband, Rebecca paused. "John," she finally said. "They said there was an accident. Someone fell off the train?"

"Actually, that was me," John explained. "Dan's all right. Saved the day, same as always."

Rebecca took a cautious step forward. "My God," she gasped as she took in the cuts and bruises. "Your face!"

Leaping into action, Rebecca gathered some water and a clean cloth. Pushing John into a nearby seat, she began to wash his wounds. As she worked, she smiled. "It's good to see you," she said. "What's it been? Nine years?"

"Eight since you stopped writing," John replied, his voice strained. He hadn't planned on seeing Rebecca so soon. And definitely not like this.

"We were just kids back then," she said softly.

Noticing the new scarf tied around Rebecca's neck, John tried to change the subject. "He takes good care of you, I see."

"In his way," Rebecca answered. She turned to get more supplies, the smile fading from her lips momentarily. If only John knew . . . Steeling herself, she continued cleaning. "He spends most of his time over in Indian territory these days."

John cocked his head. "Indian territory? Doesn't sound like my brother. Doing what?"

"Whatever it is, he doesn't talk to me about it," Rebecca answered sharply, putting an end to that conversation. "So, you got a place to stay?"

"Not as yet," John answered.

"Then you stay with us at Willow Creek," Rebecca said. She dabbed his cheek with some more water. He winced. "Look at you . . . city boy. Why would you ever want to come back here?"

John didn't say anything for a moment as he watched the emotion flicker across Rebecca's face. "It's my home," he finally answered aloud. Or at least it *was*, he added silently.

A child's voice interrupted the moment. "Who are you?" the voice asked.

Turning, John saw a young boy standing in the doorway. "Danny," Rebecca said, "this is your uncle John."

John stood up and walked over to his nephew. "How old are you?" he asked, smiling.

"Seven," Danny answered cautiously.

"You look just like your dad did when he was your age," John said, trying to sound like an uncle, even though he had no idea what *that* sounded like.

Ignoring John, Danny turned to his mother, his

expression serious. "They're going out again," he said.

Without a word, Rebecca stood up and walked out of the jailhouse. A moment later, John followed. He wasn't sure what was going on exactly, but he wanted to find out.

Behind them, in his cell, Tonto continued to chant, his body crouched low. As his chanting intensified, he raised his arms and his shadow seemed to stretch across the floor and up the walls of his cell.

✪ ✪ ✪

On Colby's main street, Dan and his rangers were saddling up. They loaded their guns, checked their supplies, and tightened the girths on their horses. Turning to retrieve his rifle, Dan saw Rebecca and John walking toward him.

"Going already?" Rebecca said when she reached his side.

Dan nodded. "If we want a chance at catching them before they hit the territories," he explained.

"I'm coming with you," John stated. "He deserves a trial."

Ignoring his younger brother, Dan turned and slid the rifle into the saddle holster. "Two rangers are dead," he said gruffly. "Didn't get no trial."

"It's the law," John insisted.

"Law looks different on the ground," Dan replied, his voice weary.

John knew he was pushing Dan's buttons, but he wasn't

about to just let Dan leave him behind. True, he hadn't been around for a long time. And true, he hadn't faced off against outlaws as his brother had. But he had learned the law. And it was his duty to follow it. "It doesn't include vengeance, no matter where you're standing," he said. He paused before quoting, " 'Wherever men unite into society—they must quit the laws of nature . . . ' "

" 'And assume the laws of men,' " another voice continued. " 'So society as a whole can prosper.' "

Turning, John saw that they had been joined by a man in an expensive suit and another man who appeared to be his assistant.

"John Locke," the man in the suit said, acknowledging the quote. "Though I never thought I'd hear the likes of it in Colby."

"Mr. Cole," Dan said, doing the introductions, "my brother, John. New county prosecutor."

"Latham Cole?" John said, reaching out his hand eagerly. "It's an honor, sir. I read about you during the war."

Cole nodded. He was used to the recognition and expected nothing less. But he hadn't come onto the dirty, dusty street for idle chitchat. Turning to Dan, he asked, "You after Cavendish?"

"Collins picked up a trail," Dan answered, nodding toward a huge bearded ranger. As they watched, the man picked something out of his beard, popped it into his mouth, and began to chew. John smiled. He had grown up with Collins and was used to his rather uncharming charms.

"Trust him?" Cole asked.

"Well enough," Dan said. "Tracked for my father."

"Make sure of it," Cole said seriously. "The railroad promised these people a hanging."

Dan paused before speaking. "Didn't know the railroad was in the business of keeping promises," he finally said.

Tension filled the air as the two men eyed each other, an unspoken argument between them. It continued for a few moments, until Cole broke it. "A simple task. Collect the prisoner, deliver him to his execution. If you're not up to that, Mr. Reid, I'll find someone who is." Tipping his hat at Rebecca, he turned and walked away, his assistant scurrying to catch up.

John watched Cole's retreating back. He didn't understand why Dan hated the other man so much. He was a war hero and clearly an important figure in town. What could have happened between the two to put them at such odds? Turning to ask, John saw that his brother and Rebecca were talking in hushed tones. As he watched, Dan turned to his son and dropped down to his eye level. He took a slingshot from his belt.

"Expect you to be bagging squirrels by the time I get

back," Dan said, placing the slingshot in his son's hands.

Danny lunged into his father's arms, fighting back tears. Dan squeezed him tight. Then he stood and mounted his horse. The other rangers did the same. Turning, he caught John's eye. "All right, Mr. Prosecutor," he said. "Let's see how your due process fares on the trail."

Reaching into a pocket, he pulled out a small object. Then he tossed it at John. Looking down, John saw it was a silver Texas Ranger badge. It was dull and scratched, the words barely legible. Flipping it over, John saw the name Reid engraved in the back. It was their father's badge. "It's Dad's," John said, almost in disbelief.

"I hereby deputize you a Texas Ranger," Dan said in all seriousness before adding, "Can't help you with them clothes."

CHAPTER 5

It was a good day for tracking outlaws. The sky was blue and cloudless and the desert floor dry. As Dan, John, and the other rangers galloped toward the foothills of a distant canyon, the horses' pounding hooves kicked up dust and dirt.

Astride his horse, John shifted in the saddle. Adjusting the brim of his hat, he noticed that there was a huge white horse pacing the group. As they entered the trees at the base of the canyon, the horse kept up, moving in and out of the sparse vegetation.

Following his brother's gaze, Dan saw the animal, too. He pulled up beside John. "Indians call that your spirit horse," he explained. "Ready to carry you to the other side."

John rolled his eyes. "You can't scare me with your ghost stories anymore." As he spoke, a beam of sun hit a silver Comanche totem Dan was wearing around his neck. "Since when did you start wearing Indian jewelry?"

"Since my kid brother became a lawyer," Dan answered.

"World needs lawyers same as it does rangers," John pointed out.

"Reckon so," his brother replied. Then, with a smirk, he added, "Nice hat, by the way. They didn't have a bigger one?" With a laugh, he kicked his horse and rode ahead, leaving John behind.

John let out a sigh. Would his brother ever think of him as anything but a little boy trailing after him? He had seen things Dan could never imagine. He had lived in a city and become a lawyer, but still, Dan just saw him as his pesky younger brother. Nothing more.

"He missed you," a voice said, interrupting John's thoughts. Turning, he saw that Collins had ridden up next to him.

"Could have fooled me," John replied bitterly. Shaking his annoyance off, he looked closely at the big man. Collins had been with Dan for years. He probably knew more about him than just about anybody. And that meant he might have an answer to the question that had been bugging John since they left Colby. "So, what is it between Mr. Cole and my brother?"

"Dan did a little work for the railroad, forcing homesteaders off their land," Collins explained. "Call it *eminent domain*. Just didn't have the taste for it. Change don't come easy for your brother."

"A man can't stay the same with the world evolving around him," John said after a moment. "No matter how much he wants to."

Collins tossed an empty bottle of whiskey over his shoulder. "That's what your daddy used to say. He saw it coming. That's why he sent you away to school." Reaching into his saddlebag, he pulled out another bottle. Noticing John's raised eyebrow, Collins shrugged. "Steadies the hand."

As the posse of rangers continued on, John stayed silent, listening to the other men chat and joke among themselves. They had an easy rapport, built from long days in the saddle and even longer nights under the cloudless, star-filled sky. Not for the first time, John wondered what he was doing there and how, or if, he'd ever fit in.

✪ ✪ ✪

The group made camp soon afterward and were up early the next morning. A short while later, they found themselves in front of the entrance to a narrow canyon known as Bryant's Gap. Two jagged white rocks jutted straight up out of the canyon, their tips piercing the bright blue sky. The rangers sat on their horses, unusually quiet.

"Could go by the flats," Navarro finally suggested.

Collins shook his head. "And lose a day. Maybe a day and a half."

"What do you figure, Dan?" Navarro asked, turning to their leader.

"Figure Collins is going to go take a look," Dan answered. "If he can stay in the saddle."

As if to prove he would have absolutely no trouble staying on, Collins let out a "Yee haw!" and spurred his horse forward. They thundered into the canyon, the sound of hoofbeats echoing off the rock walls before fading away.

Riding over to John, Dan pulled a pistol out of his waistband and held it out. John shook his head. "Don't believe in them," he said. "You know that."

"Cavendish doesn't care one way or the other," Dan pointed out.

"I'll take my chances," John said, trying not to shudder at the thought of Cavendish and his wicked grin.

Just then, a whistle echoed from the canyon's entrance. Looking up, John saw that Collins had returned and was waving them in. The coast appeared to be clear. With another wave, Collins turned and disappeared back into the shadows. Kicking his horse's sides, John followed the rest of the rangers as they entered Bryant's Gap.

Inside the canyon, the air was chillier, the sun unable to reach the floor and heat the sand like the rest of the desert. The rangers rode single file along the bed of a dried-up river as above a lone crow circled ominously. The sound of the horses' hooves echoed and bounced off the rock walls, eerie in the otherwise silent canyon. A shadow passed over the group. Nervously, the rangers unsnapped their holsters as Dan reached for his rifle. Something was off.

"Where's Collins?" Dan said.

CRACK! A single shot rang out. A moment later, Navarro fell from his saddle.

The rangers circled up just—CRACK! CRACK! CRACK!—shots began ringing out from every direction. Clayton fell, then Hollis. The gunfire continued, but the remaining rangers couldn't see who was shooting. It was like being attacked by ghosts. Breaking formation, the rangers took off.

But it was too late. In moments, Martin was shot off his horse. Then Blaine fell. As he struggled to stand, another volley of shots cut him back down. John kicked his horse, leaning low over the saddle. He could see the end of the canyon ahead. He saw Dan race through to safety. If he could just get to it . . .

Suddenly, he felt a thud, and before he knew what was

happening, his horse fell, pinning him beneath its weight. John pushed and shoved, but it was no use. The horse weighed at least a thousand pounds. He gulped as more gunfire rang out. He was as good as dead.

"Take my hand!"

Craning his neck, John saw Dan, his arm outstretched. He had come back for him! John reached out as Dan pulled him free and—

CRACK!

Dan's horse let out a wild whinny and reared up. As if in slow motion, Dan slid from the saddle and crumpled to the ground.

John scrambled over to his brother, picked up Dan's head, and cradled it in his lap. A single splotch of red slowly grew bigger on Dan's chest. He had been mortally wounded, and he knew it.

"She always loved you," Dan said, his voice weak. "Take care of her for me."

John shook his head as tears threatened to spill out of his eyes. This wasn't happening. It couldn't be happening. He had just gotten back! And Dan was the strong one. The brave Texas Ranger. He couldn't be hurt. "Just hold on," John urged, shaking his brother gently.

"You shouldn't have come back, Johnny," Dan said. "I messed up . . ."

Ignoring his brother's protests, John lifted him under the shoulders, determined to get them out of there. But before he could even take a step, there was another loud CRACK. John felt a searing pain course through his body, and then everything went dark.

⭐ ⭐ ⭐

Silence had fallen over the canyon once again. As the dust cleared, Cavendish and his gang made their way through the fallen rangers. Arriving at Dan, Cavendish paused. The ranger's breathing was shallow and his face pale as he struggled for every breath.

"You've looked better," Cavendish said, smiling cruelly.

Summoning all his strength, Dan raised himself and cursed at Cavendish.

"All heart, ain't you?" Cavendish replied, relishing his opponent's pain. Slowly, he pulled a curved blade out of his belt. "A year you took from me in that sweatbox in Tulsa. You take something from me, I'm going to take something from you. . . ."

On the ground nearby, John struggled to regain consciousness. His eyes flickered open and closed, allowing him only glimpses of what was happening. He could hear the evil in Cavendish's voice as he continued to talk to his dying brother. He could make out the outlaw as he lowered the curved blade, and saw as the other outlaws turned their heads, horrified. As John slipped into unconsciousness, the last thing he saw was Cavendish rising, a trail of blood across his brow, his hands red. With a silent cry, John let the darkness take him.

As Cavendish wiped his hands on a handkerchief, one of his men stepped forward and kneeled next to Dan's lifeless body. It was Collins. The big man had tears in his eyes. "Deal dies with you, old friend," he said softly. Reaching out, he snapped the silver totem from Dan's neck. He had shown his friend no honor in life. Perhaps he could find some way to do so in death.

But before Collins could slip the totem in his pocket, Jesus snatched it out of his hand. With a greedy smile, he jumped on his horse. A moment later, Cavendish gave the orders for everyone—including Collins—to mount up. Then he let out a loud "YA!" and the outlaw gang took off, leaving the dead rangers behind.

CHAPTER 6

The sun was high in the sky, bathing the canyon with warm light. But that was the only nice thing about the scene. Vultures had begun to arrive, circling closer and closer to the canyon. Finally, several of the vultures landed on the ground, flapped their wings, and began to hop toward the body of a ranger.

SWISH! A rock flew through the air, scattering the scavengers. A moment later, Tonto mysteriously appeared, having somehow escaped from jail. Behind him was a collection of newly dug graves. Six of them were already full. Reaching down, he grabbed the ankles of the ranger and then, as gently as possible, dragged him over to one of the empty graves.

Tonto began to chant, his voice echoing off the walls as he urged the spirits of the rangers on. Then, in the fashion of his people, he began to search their bodies. He took a pair of boots off one of the men, a silver pillbox from another, a rosary from the third. For each item he took, Tonto left something: a feather for the boots, string for the pillbox, a shell for the rosary.

The last grave was John Reid's. Noticing the shiny silver badge on John's coat, Tonto stepped into the grave and began to unpin it. Suddenly, John's hand shot out, seizing the Comanche's wrist. Startled, Tonto fell backward and began to struggle with the dead man. But the dead man's grip was surprisingly strong and Tonto couldn't get free. As he glanced around, his gaze fell on a small rock. He picked it up and with a *THUMP!* hit John on the head. Immediately, Tonto's hand was released.

Scrambling out of the grave, Tonto tried to catch his breath. John Reid was dead. He had been shot and Tonto had checked to make sure. So how had he been able to grab Tonto's arm? Glancing around nervously, Tonto shook his head. Yes, John Reid had been dead. Tonto had NOT just killed him with that rock. But to be sure, he'd bury him anyway. Quickly, he covered John with a thin layer of dirt.

Satisfied he had done the right thing, Tonto began to walk away.

He had made it only a few steps when the sound of a horse's whinny stopped him in his tracks. As he turned, Tonto's eyes grew wide. Standing there was a beautiful white horse—the very same horse that had been following the rangers earlier. It stood right in front of John's grave, holding the man's big white cowboy hat in its teeth.

Tonto dropped to his knees. He had been waiting so long for this moment. This horse had been sent there to help him; he just knew it. "Greetings, noble spirit horse," the Comanche Indian said.

As Tonto watched, the horse dropped the hat. Then, ever so gently, the horse pushed away the dirt covering John's body with its hoof, revealing the ranger star. Tonto looked at the badge, then up at the horse. This had to be a joke. The horse couldn't mean John Reid. Straight-edged, law-abiding, gun-fearing John Reid? No, there had to be some mistake.

Tonto stood up, walked over to the grave, and pointed at John. "Half-wit," he told the horse. "Wet brain." Then he led the horse to Dan's grave and pointed. "Great warrior."

The spirit horse walked back over to John's grave.

Once again, Tonto led the horse back to Dan's. And once again, the horse shook his mane and made his way back to John. This time he even licked John's face.

Tonto's shoulders dropped and he let out a sigh. The

spirit horse had spoken. And it looked like Tonto was going to have to listen, whether he liked it or not.

John's head hurt terribly. His throat was parched and his eyelids felt like they weighed a thousand pounds. For a moment, John was able to open his eyes. But only for a moment. He was able to make out a beautiful white horse and then his eyes closed again and he succumbed to the darkness.

A series of images began to appear through the darkness. There was a flash of sun and then it faded away to reveal Tonto's face, glowing red over a fire. A scorpion crawled across a series of Comanche Indian cave drawings before fading away. Once more, Tonto appeared, this time dropping a ranger badge into the fire as water began to flow over the silver. John heard the sound of horses' hooves pounding the ground, and then the air filled with the noise of a thousand locusts as they swarmed around a dead bird. John struggled and called out and then that image faded. In its place was Rebecca, her hair blowing in the breeze as it had all those years earlier. . . . And then she too was gone and Tonto appeared one last time as he poured molten silver into a bullet casing. The last thing he saw, as the darkness began to fade, was Cavendish, wiping blood across his brow.

John woke with a start. His heart was pounding and his head felt fuzzy. He began to get to his feet but fell back down, dizzy. When he was finally able to stand, he found himself on a ledge, thousands of feet in the air. John stepped back until he was pressed up against the rock wall. Seeing a path, he slowly began to make his way down.

It took him a while, but finally he got to the bottom of the path. The first thing he saw was a clearing. And in the middle of the clearing stood Tonto, talking to a large white horse. Cautiously, John approached him. Looking down, he noticed a gun lying among a pile of assorted items. He inched forward, his hand outstretched. . . .

"If you're going to sneak up on an Indian, best do it downwind," the Comanche said, startling John.

Acting quickly, John snatched up the gun. Another wave of dizziness washed over him and he shook his head, trying to clear his vision. "Why are you talking to that horse?" he asked when he could see again.

"My grandfather spoke of a time when animals could speak," Tonto answered, his back still turned to John. "When you get them alone, some still do. I cannot decide if this one is stupid, or just pretending."

John sighed. Tonto made no sense at all. Looking down, John noticed two things. One, he had no boots on. And two, he was very, very dirty. "Why am I covered in dirt?"

"Because I buried you," Tonto said as though that were obvious.

Buried him? "Then . . . why am I alive?"

Finally, Tonto turned. He moved toward John. "The horse says you're a Spirit Walker. A man who has been to the other side and returned and, therefore, cannot be killed in battle. . . ." Tonto's voice trailed off as he lifted John's hand and poured birdseed into it. "But he's just a horse."

As Tonto turned to walk away, John looked down at the seed in his hand and then at the other man. Suddenly, his eyes narrowed. "Are those my boots?" he asked.

The Comanche kept walking. There would be time for questions later. Now he needed to start a fire and get food, or else it would be a long, cold, hungry night.

⭐ ⭐ ⭐

Night had fallen and the sky was full of a thousand stars. A fire crackled near the clearing's creek as a rabbit slowly turned on a spit, roasting. Tonto had told John what had happened after he was shot in the canyon, and now the two of them sat in silence, each lost in his own thoughts.

Finally, John spoke up. "They cut out his heart," he said, his voice full of sadness and confusion. "What kind of man does something like that?"

"Not a man," Tonto corrected. "An evil spirit, born in the

empty spaces of the desert. A hunger that cannot be satisfied, with the power to throw nature out of balance." Pausing, he picked a piece of meat off the rabbit and then threw it to the edge of the clearing. A dozen more rabbits leaped out of the shadows, tearing into the meat. The Comanche's eyes grew wide and he inched closer to the fire. Noticing John was looking at him, he went on. "My people call the spirit Windigo. I am Tonto of the Comanche, last of the Windigo hunters."

"What do you want from me?" John asked, confused. What Tonto was saying sounded downright crazy.

Tonto stood up and walked over to the white horse. "A vision said a great warrior and Spirit Walker would help me on my quest," Tonto said as he reached into a saddlebag. "I would have preferred someone else. Your brother, for instance. He would have been good. But who am I to question the Great Father?"

"All I know is a man killed my brother," John said angrily. "I'll see him hang for it."

Tonto nodded. He had expected John to say something like that. "Then you will need this." He held out a silver bullet.

"A bullet?" John said, taking the small item in his hand. "A *silver bullet*?"

"Silver made him what he is," Tonto answered. "And so it will return him to the earth."

John had heard enough. He didn't need silver bullets or some crazy Comanche searching for a mythical Windigo. He needed justice. And that was not something Tonto seemed to understand. Standing up, he took Tonto's hand and placed the bullet in his palm. He closed the man's fingers around it. "You know what?" he said. "I want to thank you for everything you've done for me, but I should get back." Grabbing his boots, he began to struggle into them.

"I am also looking for Butch Cavendish," Tonto said. "I was prisoner on the train the way the coyote stalks the buffalo. After hunting twenty-six years I finally had my prey." John began to walk away, but Tonto's next words stopped him in his tracks. "Until you interfered."

Turning, John raised an eyebrow. "Actually, I think I saved your life. So we're even."

For a moment, Tonto just stared at him, a wild look in his eye. Then he reached out and—SLAP!—hit him right across the face.

"OW!" John cried out. "What was that for?"

Tonto shrugged. Then he pointed at his bird as if to say the animal had done it. "Bird angry," he said.

"Yeah, well, I can't help you," John snapped. He turned on his heel and began to walk away once more. "Or your bird."

"Where are you going?" Tonto called after him.

"Into town to form a posse," John shouted over his

shoulder. He needed to get back to Colby. Back to Rebecca and Danny. He needed to figure out his next steps before Cavendish slipped even farther away.

"Wouldn't do that, Kemosabe," Tonto said. "A greater power wanted your brother dead."

"Right, a spirit. I know."

Tonto shook his head. "There was a gun waiting for Cavendish on the train."

John stopped. Behind him Tonto was once again sitting by the fire, working a piece of leather.

"Eight men rode into the canyon," the Comanche Indian went on, not looking up. "I only dug seven graves."

A wave of realization washed over John and he felt dizzy and sick. Now he knew what Tonto was getting at. "Collins," he said softly.

Tonto nodded. "Find the traitor, you find the man who killed your brother."

Finally, John turned around, his eyes full of emotion. Tonto threw the piece of leather at his feet. Reaching down, John saw it was a piece of his brother's vest. Two bullet holes, ringed in blood, pierced the dark brown leather. While they had been talking, Tonto had fashioned it into a mask.

"Eyes cut by the bullets that killed him," Tonto said. "From the great beyond, he will protect you . . . and the ones you love."

"You want me to wear a mask?" John asked, holding up the leather.

Tonto nodded. "The men you seek think you are dead, Kemosabe. Better to stay that way."

For a moment, John said nothing. This was not what he had imagined when he had agreed to come home. But he also couldn't imagine letting his brother's death go unpunished. Finally, he spoke. "If we ride together, it's to bring these men to justice in a court of law. Is that understood?"

Picking up John's hat, Tonto knocked a crease in it. Then he held it out, as if it were a contract. "Justice is what I seek, Kemosabe. . . ."

CHAPTER 7

John had donned the mask, albeit grudgingly, and agreed that keeping his identity a secret was probably a good idea. While he didn't like it, he was the lone ranger. It was up to him to bring justice.

After following Tonto out of the clearing and through the desert, John now found himself riding through the strangest town he had ever seen. As they made their way down the street, they passed by a fire breather who blew a plume of smoke in their faces. There were doors leading to elaborate gambling halls. Bearded ladies and monkey boys stood in front of a circus tent while women of the night flaunted their wares from the windows of nearly every building. There seemed to be a distraction for every type of person. All in one place.

Shifting in his seat, the Lone Ranger reached up and adjusted the mask on his face. He had been uncomfortable before they arrived, but now he was downright miserable. "What is this place?" he asked, turning to Tonto.

"The iron horse carried you west . . . here is where it lifts its tail." Tonto pulled out his watch and tried to flick it open. As usual, the trick didn't work.

The pair continued through the town until they finally arrived in front of a tent with loud, bawdy music filtering out through its doors. The Lone Ranger could make out the shadows of people dancing, drinking, and having a good time. In front of the entrance stood a mountain of a man named Homer.

They dismounted their horses and made their way over to the big man. The Lone Ranger held out a flyer that Collins had given to him before they had left Colby. On the front was written RED'S TRAVELING ENTERTAINMENT. "We're looking for somebody," he said.

Homer glanced down at the man in the mask and the Comanche with the bird. He raised an eyebrow. Red's had a lot of things, but Homer wasn't sure it had what *these* guys were looking for. "Got money?"

"Of course," the Lone Ranger replied, reaching into his pockets. They were empty. "Actually, I seem to be a little light."

Reaching around him, Tonto handed Homer the silver pillbox he had taken from one of the rangers. Homer took it, his giant hand dwarfing the small box. It seemed to do the trick. With a flourish, Homer pulled aside the tent flaps and ushered them inside.

Nothing could have prepared the Lone Ranger for the sight that greeted him. It was a place completely dedicated to drinking, gambling, fighting, and more. Everywhere he looked, the Lone Ranger saw women laughing and dancing with railway men from all over the world. The men who worked tirelessly on the railroad by day had come here to forget about the hours of tough manual labor in the blistering hot sun. Singing, yelling, laughing, and screaming echoed throughout the bawdy room as the Lone Ranger and Tonto entered the establishment.

"The sickness of greed is strong," Tonto said solemnly as the Lone Ranger scanned the area, looking for Red.

The masked man and the Comanche continued to follow Homer through the tent and up a flight of stairs. They arrived at a balcony overlooking the entire room. "Couple freaks to see you," Homer announced.

Sitting behind a desk, Red Harrington studied her account books through a pair of wire-rimmed spectacles. In her hand she held a beaker full of a chemical concoction that she shook absentmindedly.

"Better let me do the talking," the Lone Ranger whispered to Tonto. After all, he was a lawyer. Speaking convincingly was part of the job. And a pretty woman like Red? She would probably love his charms. "Ma'am . . ." he began.

Red looked up. "What's with the mask?" she asked. She lifted her right leg and dropped it onto the desk with a loud *THUMP!* Her leg was, in actuality, an impressive prosthetic. Tonto's eyes grew wide while the Lone Ranger blushed. Ignoring the men's reactions, Red continued. "Second thought, don't answer that. One thing you learn in my business: killers, preachers, war heroes, and railroaders—every man has a thing."

The combination of "war hero" and "railroader" reminded the Lone Ranger of someone. "You referring to Mr. Cole?" he asked.

"Oh, no, not Mr. Cole," Red replied, shaking her scarlet hair. "By all reports he's no longer guided by the same imperatives as other men." As she spoke, she raised her skirt slightly, revealing more of the prosthetic leg. Tonto's eyes bulged as she adjusted her garter.

"Well, in this case, I can assure you, the mask is purely functional," the Lone Ranger said, trying to get back on track.

But Red had something else in mind. Yanking on her garter, she fired a small gun hidden in the heel of her shoe. As the Lone Ranger and Tonto jumped, a chair at the end of the bar beneath them exploded, sending a man flying. This was Red's intended target. The man who had been seated in that chair had been drinking and refused to pay and was now pawing at one of her dancers. Red had to make an example for all to see. The dancer, thankful for the intervention, smiled and waved up at Red. "Everyone pays, gentlemen!" Red announced before turning her attention back to her two guests.

Unable to help himself, Tonto leaned closer to the leg. "Scrimshaw?" he asked.

"Ivory," Red corrected.

Watching the two, the Lone Ranger let out a sigh. They were never going to get any answers if he left it up to Tonto. "We're looking for a man, name of Collins," he said. "Tracker, speaks Indian."

"Never heard of him," Red said, shrugging her pale white shoulders.

The Lone Ranger's eyes narrowed. He didn't believe her for a minute. He knew for a fact Collins had visited this establishment. Pulling back his jacket, he flashed his badge. "You know, on my way in, I happened to notice a number of fairly serious health code violations." Red didn't seem bothered. So the Lone Ranger went on. "Inadequately marked fire escapes and a fairly sinister-looking jar of pickles on the bar. I'd hate to have to shut you down."

Red raised a perfectly arched eyebrow. "Homer?" she called. "Help these morons find the door, would you?"

Tonto's eyes flashed with fury, and before the Lone Ranger knew what was happening, the Comanche Indian had stabbed a knife into Red's account book. "Windigo getting away!" he cried.

Instantly, multiple guns were pointed at their heads. Red herself held a pearl-handled revolver aimed directly at Tonto's face. "What is he talking about?" she demanded, looking at the Lone Ranger.

"Nothing," he replied, his hands in the air. "It's an Indian thing."

Tonto shook his head, furious. "Man with a taste for human flesh," he said.

There was a beat as the expression on Red's face changed from annoyed to afraid. "Butch Cavendish," she said softly.

"That's right," the Lone Ranger said.

Red uncocked and lowered the gun. "Well, why didn't you just say so?"

✪ ✪ ✪

A short while later, the Lone Ranger and Tonto found themselves in a place few men were allowed—Red's bedchamber. As she led them inside, she gave them information. "Collins was in about a week ago. With a lawman. Ranger like you, matter of fact. Said his name was Reid."

Tonto, who had been scanning the contents of Red's room with avid curiosity, looked up. Across the room, the Lone Ranger shook his head. "Dan Reid?" he asked. "You must be mistaken. He's a married man."

"Oh, we get those occasionally," Red replied, unaware of how her words stabbed at John. She went on. "Had themselves an argument. About something they found in the desert. Paid me with this." Reaching over, she dumped a rock of silver onto the table in front of her.

Tonto jumped back as though burned. "Don't touch it! Cursed!"

Rolling his eyes, the Lone Ranger picked it up. Instantly, it felt as though he had been hit by a bolt of lightning. A series of sights and sounds flashed before him. Water running over silver; Comanche Indian symbols on a cave wall; the sound of women and children screaming . . .

The Lone Ranger dropped the silver back on the table and the images disappeared. He shook his head. That had been . . . different. Noticing the man's reaction, Tonto raised an eyebrow.

Unaware of the Lone Ranger's vision, Red poured two stiff drinks. "Indian's right. It's worthless around here," she said, nodding at the silver and handing the Lone Ranger a glass. "Get it to San Francisco, they'd pay a thousand dollars cash. Maybe I'll be on the first train west. Retire."

As she spoke, Tonto poked the silver. Nothing happened. He picked it up. Still nothing. He squeezed it. Still absolutely nothing. What had John seen? And why couldn't he see it? Frustrated, Tonto dumped the silver back on the table.

Just then, there was a knock at the door and Homer poked his head in. "We got trouble," he announced.

Red looked through a peephole and saw that an angry mob of people had gathered. "I'm afraid we'll have to bring our little visit to a close," she said, turning back and eyeing Tonto. "Some of my clientele don't take kindly to an Indian on the premises."

"He has as much right to be here as anyone else," the Lone Ranger protested. "That's the law."

Red shook her head. "Not since the Comanche violated the treaty," she pointed out.

"The treaty?" the Lone Ranger repeated, confused. When had they violated the treaty?

"Didn't you hear?" Red replied. "They been raiding settlements up and down the river."

The Lone Ranger's eyes grew wide as his heart began to race. "My God," he whispered. "Rebecca . . ." They had to get out of there—now!

"Better go out the back," Red suggested, seeing the fear

in the Lone Ranger's eyes. She sat down and stretched out on a divan, her ivory leg—and the secret gun—pointed right at the door.

Making his way to the back of the room, the Lone Ranger looked up and saw a painting of Red as a young dancer. In it, she had both her legs. "How do I thank you?" the Lone Ranger asked.

Red smiled. "Just make sure that animal pays for what he took from me," she answered.

The Lone Ranger nodded. The beast had taken Red's leg and his brother's life and turned Collins into a monster. Yes, he would be happy to make Butch Cavendish pay. Very happy. But first they had to get out of there—and fast.

CHAPTER 8

As soon as Red had announced that the angry mob was after him, Tonto hightailed it out the back door. But before he left, he took a moment to sample some of the whiskey Red had so graciously poured—for the Lone Ranger. Satisfied, he once again made for the back door.

On the other side was a rickety set of stairs leading down. Weaving slightly, Tonto made his way out of Red's place, only to find himself on a side porch. In front of him stood the Lone Ranger's spirit horse. As Tonto watched, the beautiful creature leaned down and picked up a bottle of beer in his teeth. Then, just as Tonto had done moments before, the horse tilted his big head back and drank deeply.

"Nature is indeed out of balance," Tonto muttered under his breath.

Tonto could hear the sound of the mob growing closer. Turning back to the white horse, Tonto grabbed its reins and clucked. "We go," Tonto commanded. The horse didn't move. Tonto pulled on the reins harder. Still the horse did not budge. "Stubborn beast!"

Just then, there was a shout from around the corner. A moment later, another mob that had gathered appeared. They were shouting and waving their fists angrily. Throwing the reins down, Tonto began to run, the mob close behind.

Behind him, the Lone Ranger appeared at the top of the stairs. Putting two fingers in his mouth, he let out a piercing whistle. Below, the white horse raised his head and trotted to the bottom of the stairs. The Lone Ranger jumped on the banister and slid down, landing rather awkwardly in his saddle. Scrambling into position, he kicked the horse forward. The mob that had been inside Red's saw the Lone Ranger galloping off and gave chase.

The Lone Ranger and his horse raced down one alley and up another, the mob staying close on their heels. Urging the horse faster and faster, the Lone Ranger tried to find a way out of the godforsaken town of sin. But everywhere he turned there was another alley or another obstacle in his way. Finally, he and his horse careered around a corner. In front of him, he saw Tonto running wildly, his arms flapping and the feathers on his head flying. "YA!" The Lone Ranger spurred his horse on faster, catching up with Tonto. "Come on!" he said, leaning down and holding out his hand.

Tonto looked up, his eyes wild. Grabbing the Lone Ranger's hand, he swung up behind him. Aiming the horse straight ahead, the Lone Ranger and Tonto raced away from Red's and into the desert night. Behind them, the angry mobs collided and turned on each other, forgetting their original target altogether.

Looking back at the mobs, Tonto sighed. "Nature is, indeed, out of balance."

✪ ✪ ✪

At the Reid farm, Danny was unaware of his father's death and his uncle's new identity. In the late afternoon sun, he played a game of fetch with his dog, while in a nearby pasture, his mother hammered another post into the ground. The farm required constant work, and with the absence of her husband, most of the responsibility had fallen on Rebecca's small shoulders. She had wanted to get as much of the pasture fence fixed as possible before nightfall, but seeing the tired look on her farmhand's face, she put down her tools.

"Let's call it a night, Joe," she said to the exhausted farmhand.

The weathered old man nodded and headed back to his quarters, lugging various tools. For a moment, Rebecca stood still, enjoying the peace of the late afternoon. She glanced over and saw Danny and his dog and smiled. It was rare to be able to stop for even a moment. But then a noise from across the river interrupted the calm. Looking over, Rebecca saw a Comanche Indian sitting atop his horse. His dark eyes were trained on her. After a moment, he turned and rode away, disappearing from sight.

"Come on, Danny!" Rebecca called, trying to keep the fear out of her voice.

The young boy raced over and together they began to walk toward the farmhouse. As they did so, Rebecca couldn't help noticing that the usually incessant drone of insects had gone quiet. Suddenly, the dogs began to bark. Rebecca grabbed Danny's hand as she picked up the pace.

Rushing into the farmhouse, Rebecca turned and slid the heavy wooden bolt across the door. "Pilar," she said to their young Mexican maid, "get the shutters."

As Pilar began to close the heavy shutters over the windows, Rebecca walked to the fireplace. Above the mantel hung one of Dan's old rifles. With shaking fingers, Rebecca pulled it down and began to load it, trying hard not to drop it to the ground.

Behind her, Danny looked on, his eyes wide. He had never seen his mother scared before. Something bad must be coming.

Just then, the sound of gunfire rang out. Rebecca raced to one of the windows and raised the shutter slightly, giving herself a small peephole. On another wall, Danny peered out a knothole in the wood.

Out in the farmyard, a group of Comanche riders appeared, guns drawn, and they began to shoot at the harmless livestock and unsuspecting farmhands. Rebecca watched as Joe raced into the yard and began firing his pistol. But he was outnumbered. In moments, he was cut down. One of the intruders jumped down from his horse and walked over to Joe, a knife raised high. He sank to his knees beside Joe and lowered his hand.

Danny reared back from the knothole as his mother began firing her gun. But he knew it was no use. They were in serious trouble. . . .

✪ ✪ ✪

The Lone Ranger and Tonto had raced as fast as they could toward the Reid farm. Arriving at a vista overlooking the farm below, the Lone Ranger felt his heart drop. The farm was in ruins. Fires still burned where the Indians had set buildings ablaze. Dead animals and men were strewn across the yard, and in the distance, the Lone Ranger could make out the neighboring farm, fires burning through its barns and house.

"We're too late," he said, his voice full of emotion. Spurring his horse forward, he galloped down to the farm, Tonto following.

Inside the farmhouse, chairs were overturned and picture frames were charred from fire. The body of Joe, the farmhand, lay in the middle of the floor, where he had been dragged at some point. Reaching down, the Lone Ranger picked up the remains of a photograph. It was a picture of him and his brother. Rebecca stood in the middle, smiling, while the brothers tried to look serious. How could he have let this happen? First his brother, now his brother's family? He had failed them all.

Suddenly, the Lone Ranger felt a hand on his shoulder. He jumped, but it was only Tonto. The Comanche looked as unhappy as John felt. "They took them alive," he said softly.

"Indian savages," the Lone Ranger hissed.

Leaning down, Tonto took a ring from Joe's finger. "Wasn't Indians," he said.

"What are you talking about?" the Lone Ranger asked, cocking his head.

Before answering, Tonto gently laid a feather on Joe's body. "Indians make trade," he said after a moment.

"Leave him alone," the Lone Ranger said, his tone growing cold. He had known Joe all his life. He hadn't deserved to die this way, and he definitely didn't deserve to be pawed at by this crazy bird-feeding man.

Tonto ignored him and continued going through Joe's pockets. It was too much. With a cry of rage, the Lone Ranger charged at Tonto. Ducking to one side, Tonto dodged the charge and then, in one swift move, picked up the Lone Ranger and flipped him over on his back. He leaned down, a knife to the masked man's throat. "The Indian is like the coyote and leaves nothing to waste," Tonto said, his breathing steady. "Tell me, Kemosabe, why does the white man prefer killing for killing's sake?"

Before the Lone Ranger could reply, a scream pierced the air. It was coming from the barn. Withdrawing his knife, Tonto stood up and headed for the door. The Lone Ranger followed, but not before grabbing the pistol out of Joe's lifeless hand. His days of not carrying a weapon were over.

As quietly as possible, the Lone Ranger and Tonto made their way to the barn. Peering through the open door, they saw the Reid maid, Pilar, sitting on a hay bale. She was shaking like a leaf, her eyes full of fear as she stared at someone sitting in front of her. As the Lone Ranger followed

Pilar's gaze, his eyes went cold. Frank, one of Cavendish's men, was sitting on another hay bale. He was dressed like a Comanche Indian. At his feet was a trunk full of women's clothing.

"This one's nice, innit?" Frank said, picking a dress out of the trunk. Standing up, he clumsily wrapped the dress around Pilar's neck.

Sitting on the hay, Pilar continued to shake. Suddenly, she noticed the Lone Ranger and Tonto in the doorway. Following her gaze, Frank saw the two men as well. He reached for his gun as Pilar ran out of the room.

The Lone Ranger's silver badge flashed as he entered the barn. "Rebecca and Danny," he said to the outlaw. "Where are they?"

Seeing the barely contained fury in the Lone Ranger's eyes, Frank took a step back.

"Tell me where they are or I let the Indian do what he wants to you," the Lone Ranger said, nodding to Tonto.

Frank looked at the Lone Ranger and then at Tonto, who held up a rabbit's foot he had "borrowed" from Red's. Frank shivered. "What does he want to do?" he asked in a whisper.

"Use your imagination," the Lone Ranger replied.

BANG! BANG!

At the sound of the gunshots, the Lone Ranger and Tonto turned. What was going on now? A moment later, horses thundered into the yard and a voice called out, "Where are you, Frank?"

Taking advantage of the distraction, Frank darted for one of the barn's windows and jumped through it, shattering the glass and spooking the horses outside. He landed in front of Barret and Jesus, who were both astride their horses, still wearing the Comanche clothes from their earlier raid. As they eyed the other man, they passed a bottle between themselves.

"What's going on?" Barret demanded, taking a swig.

"Ra-ra-ranger," Frank stammered, pointing over his shoulder into the barn.

"What are you talking about?" Jesus said. There were no rangers. They had killed them all back in the canyon.

Frank shook his head. "Wearing some kind of mask!"

Barret had heard enough. Frank was a little loopy. They all knew that. But better to be safe than sorry. He took out his pistol and fired at an old oil lantern hanging in the barn's doorway. Then Jesus lit a torch and threw it right on the spilled oil. The barn erupted in flames. "Shoot anything that comes out," Barret said, taking another swallow from the bottle.

Now they just had to sit and wait. If the ranger was in there, he would be dead the moment he stepped outside. And if he didn't, he'd be dead anyway. Barret smiled. He liked those odds.

CHAPTER 9

Inside the barn, the Lone Ranger and Tonto exchanged worried glances. The flames were spreading fast and if they didn't get out of there soon, they would suffocate or burn. And neither man wanted to die that way.

"Go for horses, Kemosabe," Tonto said. "I cover you."

"Why me?" the Lone Ranger asked, hopping as a trail of fire began to lick at his toes.

"You have been to the other side," Tonto replied. "Spirit Walker cannot be killed."

The Lone Ranger looked at Tonto, then at the door, then at the flames growing higher and higher, and then finally back at Tonto. Spirit Walker or not, they couldn't just stand here and wait to die. Someone had to do something. And it looked like it was going to be him. Taking out his badge, he stepped closer to the window Frank had flown through a few minutes before. "Texas Ranger," he called out. "Put down your weapons and step forward with your hands up!"

CRACK! CRACK! CRACK! A series of gunshots splintered the wood all around the Lone Ranger. Darting back, he frantically patted his own body, feeling for wounds. But miraculously, he was unscathed.

"It is as I said—Spirit Walker," Tonto said in awe. It seemed he had been right. Which was, in hindsight, a good thing for the Lone Ranger.

But either way, they were still in trouble. The flames were growing higher and getting hotter. Outside, they could hear the outlaws reloading. Smoke was filling the air and the Lone Ranger and Tonto began to cough.

Suddenly, there was a clattering on the roof of the barn, as though something big was walking around. Tonto walked over to the large furnace used by the blacksmith, and peered in and up. His eyes grew wide. Far above, flashing bright in the moonlight, was the big white horse. Seeing Tonto, the horse bared its teeth and then let out a loud whinny. Pulling back, Tonto shook his head.

Noticing Tonto's expression, the Lone Ranger moved a step closer. "What is it?"

Gulping, Tonto told him what he had seen. For a

moment, the Lone Ranger looked disbelieving. But then he shook his head. Stranger things had happened to him. Well, at least recently, stranger things had happened. So why not a horse on a roof? With a nod, the Lone Ranger made his way over to the ladder that led to the hayloft. He quickly climbed up it and then out onto the roof through a small hatch. Bursting into the fresh air, he came face-to-face with the white horse.

"Hi . . . uh, thanks for coming," the Lone Ranger said. Behind him, Tonto climbed out onto the roof. "So, the horse? It can fly?"

"Don't be stupid," Tonto replied. Horses could talk, true. But fly? That was plain silly.

As the barn began to shudder, the Lone Ranger and Tonto hopped onto the animal's back. Turning the horse, the Lone Ranger steered him to the far end of the roof. He took a deep breath and then . . . "YAAAA!" With a cry, he kicked the animal forward. The horse's hooves echoed in the night as it galloped toward the edge of the barn. When it reached the edge, the horse reared back, and with a mighty surge of its powerful hindquarters, it jumped. The Lone Ranger and Tonto sailed over the outlaws' heads, landing silently a few feet beyond them.

In front of the barn, Barret and Jesus passed their bottle as they watched the flames consume everything. No one had come out. And no one could have survived that inferno. It looked like they were in the clear.

"Turn around," a voice said behind them. "Real slow."

Barret and Jesus did as they were told. They found themselves looking down the barrel of the Lone Ranger's gun. Beside him, Tonto weaved his knife back and forth. In the background, the white horse snorted and pawed the ground.

"Rebecca and Danny," the Lone Ranger said, his voice icy. "Where are they?"

"Comanche don't take prisoners," Barret sneered, revealing foul, rotten teeth.

Jesus nodded. "Just scalps," he added, and the two men began to laugh.

The Lone Ranger was not amused. "Feathers and war paint. You insult the Comanche name," he said, nodding at their outfits.

Beside him, Tonto nodded.

Then the Lone Ranger went on. "For they may be a simple, backward people . . ."

Tonto turned and raised an eyebrow. *Now hold on just one minute. That was uncalled for.*

". . . slave to superstition, the worship of birds and talking animals," the Lone Ranger continued, ignoring Tonto's glare. "They may live in trees, bathe in their own waste, oblivious

The Lone Ranger and Tonto. Find out how this masked man turned from a man of law into a legend of justice.

The notorious outlaw Butch Cavendish is being transported back to Texas to stand trial . . . but Cavendish has other plans.

The evil Cavendish gang breaks Butch out of the prison car of a moving train before the Texas Rangers can take him to jail.

After lawman John Reid attempts—and fails—to stop Cavendish's escape, he is captured and chained to Tonto, who is also a prisoner on this train.

After a dangerous escape from a moving train, John returns home to Texas and to his old flame, Rebecca, who is now married to John's brother, Texas Ranger Dan Reid.

After John and the rangers are ambushed by the Cavendish gang and
left for dead, a white spirit horse signals Tonto that one man—John
Reid—needs to be rescued. Tonto listens to the horse but
still thinks he rescued the wrong brother.

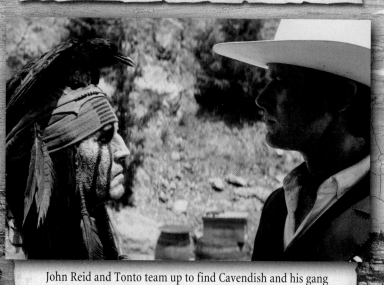

John Reid and Tonto team up to find Cavendish and his gang
and bring them to justice, but Tonto has his own plans for
"Windigo" Butch Cavendish.

The Lone Ranger and Tonto travel to meet Red Harrington, in the hope that she can lead them to Cavendish.

Meanwhile, Cavendish's gang masquerades as a group of Comanche and attacks the Reid family farm.

The Lone Ranger and Tonto race against time to find the Sleeping Man mountain—and stop Cavendish once and for all!

After capturing Butch Cavendish, the Lone Ranger must now transport him across the desert and back to Texas to face justice . . . but Butch doesn't stay captive for long.

A celebration for the completion of the Transcontinental Railroad
quickly turns to chaos as the final battle between good
and evil breaks out!

The Lone Ranger and his spirit horse, Silver, ride into action!

Having finally defeated Cavendish and his gang, the Lone Ranger and Tonto vow always to ride for justice.

to the assault on our olfactory senses. But I tell you this . . ." He paused and nodded in Tonto's direction. "That noble savage is a better man than any of you." Proud of his speech, the Lone Ranger turned to Tonto.

SLAP! Tonto hit him across the face.

"Sure about that?" Barret said, laughing.

Tonto shook his head. Then he pointed at his winged companion. "Actually," he said, eyeing the Lone Ranger apologetically, "that was the bird."

The outlaws had heard enough. Clearly the masked man and the Comanche Indian were no threat to them. They could barely stand each other. It was time to put an end to this little get-together. Dropping his bottle on the ground, Barret slowly reached for his weapon as he and Jesus spread out.

The Lone Ranger waved his gun back and forth between the two outlaws, unable to keep it on just one man.

"I take the Spaniard," Tonto said under his breath.

Clutching his gun, the Lone Ranger nodded. He hesitated. "I haven't fired a gun in nine years," he finally said in a rush.

Tonto raised an eyebrow. "I would keep that to yourself, Kemosabe," he whispered as he crouched lower and began to bob and weave.

The four men stood in a face-off. Barret's finger twitched on the trigger as Jesus aimed at Tonto's heart. The

Lone Ranger swallowed nervously while beside him Tonto narrowed his eyes and then . . .

SWISH! The Indian's knife flew through the air, ripping into Jesus's arm. The Mexican let out a scream and dropped his weapon. Seeing his chance, the Lone Ranger fired.

His bullet hit Barret's gun hand, causing the outlaw to pull the trigger. As the Lone Ranger watched, eyes wide, the bullet hit the weather vane on top of the nearby silo and flew back down toward the ground. Then it bounced off the blade of a shovel propped up against the barn, and whizzed over Tonto's head and then right into a winch in the still smothering hayloft. With a groan, the winch snapped, releasing a huge piece of timber that flew down and with a loud *CRACK!* hit the two outlaws in the head, killing them instantly.

For a moment, neither the Lone Ranger nor Tonto said anything. What had just happened had been rather, well, unbelievable. Finally, Tonto nodded. "Great shot," he said.

"Actually," the Lone Ranger said, wiping a sweaty palm on his leg, "that was supposed to be a warning shot."

"In that case, not so good," Tonto said as he began to walk over to the bodies.

Glancing at the Comanche, the Lone Ranger bit his lip. Tonto's bird hung limply from his head. It appeared the outlaws hadn't been the only ones caught in the cross fire.

Noticing the Lone Ranger's look, Tonto raised an eyebrow. "What?" he asked.

"Nothing," the Lone Ranger replied, shaking his head.

With a shrug, Tonto began to search the bodies. From around Jesus's neck he took a totem; it was the same totem that Dan Reid had once worn. Holding it, he muttered an incantation in Comanche. When that was done, he moved on to Barret. But the Lone Ranger had seen the totem.

"It was my brother's," he said, reaching out.

Tonto shook his head. "No. Comanche. Very holy."

As Tonto continued to trade with the dead men, the Lone Ranger looked across the farm. They had managed to destroy some of Cavendish's men, but there were still more out there. Including Collins. And the outlaws still had Rebecca and Danny. How were they ever going to find them now?

When he mentioned it, Tonto simply nodded. "Tracks lead north toward Indian country," he said, pointing at the hoofprints that led away from the farm.

"Four hundred square miles over rock and desert," the Lone Ranger pointed out. "Even an Indian can't track that."

"So we follow the horse, Kemosabe." Reaching out, Tonto slapped Barret's horse on its rump. It reared up and then took off, racing into the desert, its coat gleaming in the moonlight.

With a sigh, the Lone Ranger began to walk. Beside him, Tonto adjusted the lifeless bird on his head. "Kemosabe? Why do you keep calling me that?" the Lone Ranger asked. "What does it mean?"

"Wrong brother," Tonto replied simply. Picking up his pace, he walked on by.

Behind him, the Lone Ranger nodded, resigned. The Comanche was probably right. But until they found Rebecca and Danny and arrested Collins and Cavendish, he wasn't going to give up his quest for justice.

CHAPTER 10

Above a rocky pool, clouds drifted through a blue sky, casting shadows on the ground below. The water was calm, its surface a clear reflection of the sky.

Suddenly, the reflection was shattered as a man jumped into the pool. The water rippled and splashed over the sandy shore as Skinny, one of Cavendish's men, floundered about, hooting and hollering. Nearby, Cavendish's other men lowered their faces to the water, eagerly washing off their war paint.

As far from the men as she could get, Rebecca Reid knelt down and cupped her hand. She scooped up some water and held it to her son's parched lips. Danny drank eagerly, his slender body shaking.

"Pretty as they say, aren't you," a deep voice said from behind Rebecca.

Turning, she saw Cavendish staring down at her. "My husband will kill you for this," she said, pulling Danny closer to her.

Around her, the men snickered. Rebecca looked at them one by one, trying to figure out what was going on. And then Cavendish spoke, his words breaking her heart.

"That'd be a trick," he said, smiling cruelly. "Last time I saw your husband he was drowning in his own blood. I'd like to say he died well. Truth is, he begged like a dog."

Rebecca felt the blood drain from her face as, beside her, Danny's eyes filled with tears. Every time Dan had ridden off, Rebecca had lived with the fear that he would never return. But he always had. And now this man, this monster, had made her worst nightmare come true. With a cry, Rebecca stood up and lunged at Cavendish, scratching her nails down his face.

Pushing her off him, Cavendish reached up and touched the wound. His fingers came away bloody. Furious, Cavendish drew his knife. No woman was worth the trouble. He lifted the weapon and was about to bring it down when . . .

NEIGH!

The sound of a horse stopped him. Cavendish turned, ready for a fight. But it was only Frank.

The man rode into the clearing, breathing heavily. Falling from his horse, he grabbed the nearest bottle and drank thirstily. His hand shook as the liquid poured down his throat.

"Where's Barrett and Jesus?" Cavendish asked.

Wiping liquid from his chin, Frank looked up. "Killed 'em," he said, his voice trembling. "Straight draw, fired one bullet. They didn't stand a chance."

"Who killed 'em?" Cavendish asked, stepping closer.

Frank shrank back. "Wore a mask," he said. "Riding a white horse."

Cavendish narrowed his eyes. Frank was making less sense than usual. Drawing his gun, Cavendish aimed it between Frank's eyes. "Better start talking straight. Now, who killed 'em?"

"He was a ranger, Butch," Frank stammered. "A lone ranger."

The man had clearly been in the sun for too long. There were no rangers left. His whole gang knew it. They had killed them all.

But Frank went on. "Ghost of Dan Reid. Said he's coming for you. Shouldn't have done what you did."

Butch had had enough. "Shut up!" he snarled as he violently backhanded Frank, sending him flying. Around him, the other men exchanged worried looks. "Let him come. Killed him once, won't have to answer for it when I kill him again."

Rebecca saw the fear in the outlaws' eyes and the anger in Cavendish's. It made her brave and she stepped forward. "Scared, aren't you?" she said. Whipping around, Cavendish let out a growl. "You should be," she replied.

Cavendish didn't respond right away. Instead, he flipped open his gun to check the bullets and then closed it. He spun the chamber. Only then did he look up, the anger gone, once again replaced with evil. "Know what the Indians call this place?" he asked. Rebecca shook her head. "Valley of Tears. Hey, Collins."

The traitorous tracker had been sitting apart from the others, his head hung low. At the sound of his name, he looked up. Cavendish was holding out his gun, a mean smile on his lips. "I want you to take these two out there behind that rock . . . and I want you to kill them both."

"I ain't doing it," Collins said, shaking his head.

Cavendish flipped the gun in his hand so it was now pointing at Collins. "You got paid," he said. "You go all the way, or you get off here."

Collins looked at the gun and then at Rebecca and Danny. Slowly, he got to his feet. Taking the gun from Cavendish, he gestured to the prisoners. With Collins's gun at their backs, Rebecca and Danny began to walk.

✪ ✪ ✪

The three made their way through ancient rock formations, past dusty plants and old bones. Finally, they came to a hill. All around them were signs of death and decay. Valley of Tears was an appropriate name for the sad and empty place.

"That's far enough," Collins said.

Rebecca and Danny stopped. Collins came up behind them, gun raised. Slowly, Rebecca turned, pulling her son close. She stared at Collins. This was the man her husband had trusted with his life. The man Dan's father had trusted with his life. And yet here he was, about to kill them both. And for what? Money given to him by a horrible outlaw. Pity filled Rebecca's eyes and Collins looked away.

"Don't look at me," he said.

"He loved you," Rebecca replied simply.

The words hit home and Collins winced. "I said, don't look at me."

She turned away. Holding Danny tightly, she braced herself. The wind whistled through the rocks and then—

BANG! BANG!

Rebecca flinched, ready for the pain to follow the shots. But no pain came. Opening her eyes, she saw that Collins had fired the gun—at the dirt.

"Run," he said. When she hesitated, he pushed her. "Please, run!"

This time, Rebecca didn't hesitate. She grabbed Danny's hand, and they began to sprint down the rocky hill, slipping and sliding as it became steeper and steeper. Suddenly, Rebecca lost her footing and fell, landing hard and splitting open her brow. Danny bent down and tried to lift her, but he was too weak. They both fell back to the ground. Stifling a cry, the young boy looked around for something, anything, to help him. And then he heard the rhythmic pounding of hoofbeats.

His eyes grew wide as a rider raced up to them. There was a bang! And behind them, Collins fell back, dead.

Danny let out a sigh of relief. They had been saved . . . but by whom?

CHAPTER 11

The Lone Ranger was so thirsty. They had been following Barret's horse for what felt like an eternity, and still seemed no closer to finding Cavendish. His feet were blistered, his lips were parched, and his head ached. Beside him, Tonto staggered along, hiding from the burning sun underneath a pink parasol he had taken from Frank.

"Why would Cavendish make it look like Comanche violated the treaty?" the Lone Ranger asked, breaking the silence. The question had been bothering him ever since they had left the farm.

"Perhaps he wanted us to *think* Comanche violated the treaty," Tonto replied. As the Lone Ranger rolled his eyes at the very *un*helpful answer, Tonto pulled out his watch and once again tried to flip it open. Once again, the trick did not work.

"Something to do with what my brother found in the desert?" the Lone Ranger said, more to himself than to Tonto.

But Tonto replied anyway. "Perhaps," he said. "Real question is what they want with Rebecca and Danny."

"I don't want to think about that," the Lone Ranger said, trying to put an end to the conversation.

Tonto ignored the hint. "I figure Windigo wants what all creatures want." Despite himself, the ranger looked over. "To pass on its seed. But, if I were you, I would be more concerned about the boy."

Why wouldn't he just stop speaking? Every single thing he said made the Lone Ranger feel sick.

Tonto went on. "A young heart is open to the Windigo. He will try to make him a creature like himself."

"You know, you're not helping," the Lone Ranger said, picking up the pace to try to put distance between himself and the Comanche. He needed to be alone with his thoughts. He strode forward, ignoring the pain in his feet. But after a few steps, he realized Tonto wasn't even bothering to catch up. Turning around, he saw that Tonto and the horse had stopped walking. "What is it now?"

Lifting his nose in the air, Tonto took a big sniff. Unsure

what to do, the Lone Ranger did the same thing. He didn't smell anything. Then Tonto turned and looked at Barret's horse, as if waiting for an answer from the creature.

In reply, the horse swayed. Then it let out a loud groan. And then, as the Lone Ranger watched in horror, it fell over, dead.

"Now what?" the Lone Ranger asked. They had been following the horse the whole time. How were they supposed to know where to go without it? They were surrounded by flat, relentless desert. There were no street signs to guide them or places to stop and ask for directions.

Tonto shrugged.

It was the last straw. The Lone Ranger lost it. "We're lost, aren't we?" he said, his voice rising. "I knew it! Follow the horse. That was *your* idea. But you can't talk to a dead horse, can you? Here, let me try." He leaned over. "Hello? Just point the direction and we'll take it from here. What's that? Nothing?"

Pausing to catch his breath, the Lone Ranger glared at Tonto, who was calmly trying to feed his dead bird. But the seed just blew away in the wind. The ranger continued his rant. "Well, that's just terrific, isn't it? Cavendish is out there somewhere right now doing God knows what to Rebecca and Danny and I'm going to die here in the desert with you and THAT RIDICULOUS BIRD!"

Tonto didn't reply. Instead, he began to pace through the sand. He stopped, bent down, and picked up some of the dirt. He sniffed it before dropping it and then continued his pacing. Finally, he looked at the ranger. "The woman Rebecca," he said, "you will make her your squaw?" The Lone Ranger looked at him blankly. What was Tonto talking about? Rebecca was his brother's wife. He could never marry her. Tonto went on. "You spoke of her in your vision. When you were on the other side, you did not see things?"

Clearly, the sun had gone to Tonto's head. "Lack of oxygen to the brain causes hallucinations," the Lone Ranger replied. "Everyone knows that."

"Either way," Tonto said, shrugging. "You did not speak of her as the wife of your brother."

Groaning, the Lone Ranger attempted to explain the rules of polite society—which included not marrying your brother's wife. Although, he had to admit, she technically was his widow. But still, it just wasn't done! As the Lone Ranger rambled on, Tonto continued his odd pacing. He licked his finger and dipped it in the sand. Then he tasted it.

"Would you STOP!" the Lone Ranger shouted. "If you could track, we wouldn't be out here in the first place!"

Tonto ignored the ranger and squatted down, examining the ground closely. "Track," he said, looking up.

"Impossible," the Lone Ranger said. But as he watched,

Tonto took out a knife, flipped it in his palm, and then tapped the butt end against the desert floor.

PING!

The Lone Ranger's eyes grew wide. Tonto hadn't meant track as in footsteps; he had meant track as in railroad. But what was a track doing all the way out here?

The two men exchanged confused looks.

Before they could discuss it, there was a low whistle. A moment later, an arrow pierced the Lone Ranger's shoulder, and with a cry he fell to the ground.

✪ ✪ ✪

The Lone Ranger awoke with a start. Shaking his head to clear his vision, he saw that he was in a cage . . . with Tonto. Nearby a group of Comanche Indian warriors danced around a fire. Their chants echoed through the night, sending shivers down the Lone Ranger's spine.

The movement sent a surge of pain down his shoulder and he suddenly remembered—he'd been shot. Glancing down, he saw the arrow was still there. Reaching over, Tonto grabbed the free end of the arrow and pulled.

"Ahh!" shouted the Lone Ranger as the projectile slid out. "My God, that hurts! I thought you said I couldn't get shot."

"Thought so, too," Tonto replied.

The Lone Ranger sighed. Helpful, as usual. Figuring Tonto would be able to actually answer his next question, the Lone Ranger nodded at the dancing Comanche. "Apache?"

"Comanche," Tonto corrected.

"That's good, right?" the Lone Ranger said, brightening. It was about time they had a bit of good luck.

But then Tonto shook his head. "Not so much," he said, taking out a needle and a piece of thread. He began to stitch the ranger's arm. As he worked, he explained they were doing the death dance. "They are preparing for war with the white man."

"War?" the Lone Ranger repeated. Then he realized what Tonto was doing to his arm. "Wait, is that sterile?"

Tonto shot him a look. "Yes," he replied as though it were obvious. Then he added, "I make urine on it."

As Tonto jabbed the needle in for another stitch, the Lone Ranger groaned. How much worse could things possibly get?

INTERLUDE—San Francisco

Inside the Wild West tent, Will stopped Tonto. He had been listening intently to the elderly Tonto's story, but now he was confused.

"War?" he repeated. "But the Comanche didn't attack the settlements!"

Inside the diorama, Tonto danced his version of the death dance, his motions slow with age. In each hand, he held a black feather. "White man does not know this," he replied between chants.

"But you're going to tell them. . . ." Will stopped himself. He had gotten so caught up in the story he had forgotten that all this had happened long, long before. If it had happened at all. "I mean, you *did* tell them, right?"

Tonto stopped dancing, his watery eyes meeting Will's young ones. For a moment, his face was filled with great sadness. And then he simply said, "Once iron horse starts, very difficult to stop."

CHAPTER 12

Latham Cole was extremely satisfied. Everything was going exactly as planned. All around him men were busy constructing a huge bridge that would span the Hawk River. Once that was complete, there would be nothing standing in his way, or rather the railroad's way, of conquering the West. He had just a few more things to take care of. . . .

Addressing the crowd of newspapermen who had gathered, Cole spoke. "When I was a surveyor just starting out in this business, I was lost in the desert, left for dead. It was there that God appeared before me and told me to build this great railroad. To unite this great country, so no man could ever tear it asunder." He paused, letting his words sink in. "Let the Comanche make no mistake! We will NOT be dissuaded from our task. From here on, all treaties with the Indian Nation are null and void. We will be in Promontory Summit ahead of schedule. Three days from today."

With a wave, Cole made his way through the cheering crowd and headed toward the construction. He stopped to sign documents, inspect blueprints, and talk with some of the foremen. Finally, he came upon a covered wagon. Pulling back the tarp, he looked inside. Dozens of cases marked HIGHLY VOLATILE were nestled inside.

"Arrived last night," said Cole's assistant, Wendell, joining him. He nodded at the nitrate explosives.

"Put it somewhere safe," Cole said, dropping the tarp back in place. Pulling out his watch, he flipped it open just as the sound of fifty horsemen echoed through the construction site.

The Seventh Cavalry, led by Captain J. Fuller, had arrived. At Fuller's side was a Tonkawa scout wearing a cavalry uniform. "I understand you have an Indian problem," Fuller said in way of greeting.

Flipping his watch closed, Cole looked at the captain and nodded. "About time."

✪ ✪ ✪

Things had definitely gotten worse for the Lone Ranger. After being stitched up by a dodgy needle, he had been dragged unceremoniously out of his cage and into a huge teepee. He had been brought to the fire and then forced to his knees in front of Chief Big Bear and his elders. Red Knee, a great Comanche warrior, stood nearby, his cold eyes trained on the two prisoners.

The Lone Ranger swallowed nervously. Then he did what he did whenever he didn't know what else to do—he began to talk. "My name's John Reid. I know you didn't attack those settlements. If you let me go, I can prove it. There doesn't have to be a war. Understand?" Squinting, he peered through the smoke-filled air to see if the chief or elders had understood. But each man's face was stonier than the last.

"I come in peace," he went on, holding his hands to his heart. Then he began walking his fingers through the sand. "Me, Spirit Walker. From great beyond." He drew back an imaginary bow. "Hunter of Windigo . . . and other things."

Chief Big Bear turned to Red Knee and raised an eyebrow. "Sunstroke?" he asked in their native tongue.

Red Knee shrugged. "Or his mind is poisoned with whiskey."

Turning back to the Lone Ranger, Chief Big Bear spoke again, this time in English. "He told you to wear the mask," the chief said, referring to Tonto. The Lone Ranger nodded and Chief Big Bear burst into laughter. The rest of the elders did the same.

"That's funny?" the Lone Ranger asked, confused.

"Very funny," Chief Big Bear and Red Knee said at the same time, still laughing.

"Tonto is Comanche," the Lone Ranger protested. "One of you."

Getting himself under control, Chief Big Bear shook his head. "No more." Putting on a pair of wire-framed glasses, he pulled out a knife. The Lone Ranger shrank back. But instead of using it on him, the chief used it to open Tonto's pocket watch. "His mind is broken. He is . . . a band apart."

As the chief stared at the watch, the fire seemed to fade away and the Lone Ranger found himself listening to a story from a different time.

"Many moons ago, a boy found two white men in the desert." As the chief spoke, the Lone Ranger imagined a young Comanche boy coming upon two men, their skin cracked and blistered from the sun. "He brought them to his village to be healed. When they found silver in the river, they asked the boy where it came from."

In his head, the Lone Ranger saw the naive young boy pointing up the river, eager to impress the white men. One of them pulled out a watch and magically flipped it open as the boy spoke. In exchange for the cheap pocket watch, the boy agreed to bring the men to the source of the silver— a mountain shaped like a sleeping man. From high on the mountain, water fell into a river filled with more silver than any white man had ever seen or could imagine.

Chief Big Bear went on. "They took what they could carry. But they wanted to keep the place a secret so they could one day return." Once more an image flashed through the Lone Ranger's mind: the young Comanche boy walking through bodies strewn everywhere, his heart breaking. The river running red with blood. "The boy could not live with what he'd done. So he decided the men were possessed by evil spirits in the silver. Called it Windigo, like the ghost stories we tell our children to make them sleep. And he made a vow. When he found these two men, he would drain their blood into the soil of his ancestors so he could return to the tribe."

The chief's voice trailed off and the Lone Ranger shook his head, trying to clear the gruesome images from his mind. "The boy," the Lone Ranger began. "He was Tonto?"

Snapping shut the pocket watch, the chief nodded and picked up another item. It was Dan's totem. "And you are John Reid. Brother of Dan?"

"Yes, that's right," the Lone Ranger replied.

The chief looked at him thoughtfully. "By this totem, your brother swore if we kept the peace, he would protect our land. Now the cavalry cut down our children. Like all white men, your brother lied."

"No!" the Lone Ranger shouted. Catching himself, he

lowered his voice. "Dan was murdered. Let me go and I'll keep his promises."

Chief Big Bear held up the totem, studying it in the flickering firelight. The Lone Ranger watched. The silence stretched on. Finally, the Lone Ranger couldn't take it anymore. "So, do we have a deal?" he asked.

The chief paused and the Lone Ranger felt a surge of hope. But it was short-lived. "Not so much," Chief Big Bear answered.

✪ ✪ ✪

A short time later, the Lone Ranger found himself buried up to his neck in the warm desert sand. Tonto was beside him, also buried. As they watched, the Comanche warriors mounted their horses. Their faces were painted and their weapons were sharpened. From a ridge, a Comanche scout signaled as, behind him, a cloud of dust rose in the air. The enemy was approaching. It was time for war.

"My name come up?" Tonto asked out of the corner of his mouth as a horse walked past, nearly trampling him.

The Lone Ranger rolled his eyes. Seeing the chief approaching, the Lone Ranger called out. "Please!" he begged. "This is a mistake. There doesn't need to be a war."

Astride his horse, Chief Big Bear looked even bigger and more imposing than he had on the ground. He looked at the two men and then down at the watch and totem in his hand. "Makes no difference," he said, tossing the items to the ground. "We are already ghosts."

Then, as the Lone Ranger and Tonto watched helplessly, the Comanche galloped off, the sounds of the war whoops and yells quickly fading. Buried in the ground, with no chance of escape, the Lone Ranger let out a sigh. He couldn't begin to guess what would come next. But something told him he wouldn't like it.

As the dust cleared and silence fell upon the abandoned Comanche camp, the Lone Ranger and Tonto ignored each other. The Lone Ranger was still reeling from the story he had heard, while Tonto was aware something had been said to make him look bad. And both were rather unhappy to be buried up to their necks in dirt.

Just when the silence seemed like it had stretched on forever, the ground began to shake. Then in the distance came the faint sound of a trumpet. Twisting his head as far as he could, Tonto narrowed his eyes. "Cavalry," he said.

"Thank God," the Lone Ranger said, breathing a sigh of relief.

But no sooner were the words out of his mouth than the cavalry appeared, racing through the empty camp. Men shot their guns into the air as their horses raced right into teepees, trampling them to the ground.

"Over here!" the Lone Ranger shouted. "Help!"

The cavalry continued coming—but now they were coming right at them! In all the chaos, they couldn't see the two buried men. They were going to be trampled! Under the dirt, the Lone Ranger struggled to move his arms, but it was to no avail. As the horses pounded closer and closer, he closed his eyes. This was the end. . . .

Slowly, the Lone Ranger opened his eyes. The sound of the cavalry was fading, and each of the men's faces was covered in a thick layer of dirt. "Perhaps they didn't see us," the Lone Ranger suggested after a moment.

"Probably double back any minute," Tonto agreed. "Could be worse."

The Lone Ranger raised one eyebrow. "Worse?" he repeated. "How could it possibly be worse?"

"We have each other," Tonto replied flatly.

"I'm not talking to you anymore," the Lone Ranger said, turning his head. But the silent treatment didn't last long. Hearing something, he raised his head in alarm. "What is that?"

"You hear it too?" Tonto asked.

Both men grew silent, straining to make sense of the strange noise that was coming from nearby. It sounded almost like something was scratching its way out of the sand. Then, mere inches from their faces, the pocket watch and totem began to vibrate. To their horror, a large scorpion appeared, its tail raised.

"I was hoping it was in my head," Tonto said, eyeing the insect nervously. Six more scorpions dug their way out and began crawling toward the helpless men. "Nature is indeed—"

"Don't say it," the Lone Ranger hissed.

One of the larger scorpions had made it up to Tonto's face. Slowly, it began to crawl toward his nose. Beside him, the Lone Ranger blew frantically, trying to knock the scorpion loose. But it was no use. The creature's tail pulled back and . . .

A shadow fell over the trapped men, and the Lone Ranger yelped. It was the white spirit horse! Leaning down, the big animal snapped the scorpion up with its teeth and then bit down. It reached for another as the rest of the scorpions burrowed back into the safety of the dirt.

"Yes!" the Lone Ranger cried. "That a boy!"

The horse nodded its head as if to say *You're welcome.* Then it flipped its head up and down, causing the reins to fall beside the Lone Ranger. Grabbing the reins in its teeth, the horse slowly began to back up, pulling the Lone Ranger free of the dirt.

For a moment, the Lone Ranger just lay there, taking in deep breaths of air and moving his arms and legs to regain feeling. Then he got to his feet and swung up and onto the horse's back.

Still buried, Tonto looked up. "Going, Kemosabe?"

"Yes, I am," the Lone Ranger replied. He knew that he should free Tonto. That he had never intentionally tried to harm him. But still, it would probably be easier to ride alone.

"To find Rebecca and Danny?" Tonto went on. The Lone Ranger nodded. "To capture Cavendish where the river begins?"

"Exactly," the Lone Ranger replied.

Tonto nodded thoughtfully. Then he simply said, "It's a good day to die."

"Yes, well, same to you." Kicking his horse, the Lone Ranger cantered off. Glancing over his shoulder, he saw Tonto's head grow smaller and smaller. He sighed. He shouldn't feel bad. He had to do what was right. He had to save Rebecca and Danny and he had to find Cavendish. . . .

With a groan, the Lone Ranger pulled up his horse. He had just realized he couldn't leave without Tonto. Spurring the horse, he raced back into the camp. The Comanche looked up at him as though he had expected him to return. "Where the river begins," the Lone Ranger said. "You know where that is, don't you?"

Tonto nodded.

The Lone Ranger sighed. It looked like they were sticking together for a little while longer.

CHAPTER 13

Tonto held the totem that Dan Reid used to wear around his neck, and inspected it. While others saw this as just an ornate charm, Tonto saw it for what it *really* was: a map to the Sleeping Man. Tonto studied the totem and led the Lone Ranger through the rocky terrain until, finally, they were at their destination.

The Sleeping Man rose out of the desert, casting long shadows on sand and dirt below. Around its peak, birds circled, searching for prey, while on the ground animals scurried between the sparse shrubbery. But over the sounds of bird and animal calls came the distinct noise of man.

Near the top of the mountain, a mine had been dug, its various entrances now alive with activity. Workers made their way in and out of the main mine shaft, pushing carts along a track, while others carried baskets that dripped mud. Nearby, more workers stood at sorting tables, picking out silver from the harvested rocks. It was an efficient operation and it had been going on continuously for a long time.

In the middle of it all sat Butch Cavendish. He was holding a rock of silver up to the sun as Skinny nervously shaved the leader's face. At the sound of shouting, Skinny's hand slipped and the razor nicked Cavendish.

Lightning fast, Cavendish snatched Skinny's wrist, gripping it hard. "Was an accident, Butch," Skinny said, trying to pull his hand free. "Didn't mean it."

There was a beat as Cavendish pondered what to do. Finally, he let go. "What is that god-awful noise?"

Near the main mine shaft, Ray, another one of Cavendish's men, was negotiating with a group of workers. The men looked frightened and were gesturing wildly. They pointed to the mine and then at each other. Walking over, Ray ran a hand through his hair. "Sorry, Butch," he said. "Say they won't go inside no more. Indian spirits, or something. Say they causing the cave-ins."

Cavendish narrowed his gaze at one of the workers who stood apart from the others. "He the one doing the talking?"

"That's right," Ray said, nodding.

Without another word, Cavendish stood up, walked

over to the man, and shot him. The other workers fell silent. "Anybody else wanna negotiate?" Cavendish asked, holding up his gun. When no one said anything, he turned to Frank. "Now go show 'em there's nothing to be afraid of."

Frank hesitated. "I've been thinking, Butch," he said, his voice weak. "Maybe we should just take what we can carry and get out of here. We already rich, right?"

A dangerous look flashed in Cavendish's eye. He had been waiting twenty years to get his hands on the silver in Sleeping Man. He was not about to give up just because a few workers were scared of ghosts. Picking up a piece of silver, he began to hit Frank until the man lost his footing and fell to the ground. Cavendish drew his gun.

"We're taking all of it," he snarled at the cowering Frank. "Every single piece. Now get in there before I put a hole in you."

Scrambling to his feet, Frank dashed into the mine, more scared of Cavendish than the ghosts.

✪ ✪ ✪

Unbeknownst to Cavendish or his men, there *was* something other than silver in the mine. The Lone Ranger and Tonto had made their way inside under cover of dark and had been waiting for their moment to strike. The moment had arrived.

From the shadows, Tonto watched as Frank tentatively

made his way into the tunnel. He stepped closer, his face illuminated by the lantern. And then Tonto blew the light out.

Outside, Cavendish and his men heard an ear-piercing shriek. "Frank?" Cavendish called out. No reply. He nodded at Ray and Skinny to go after him.

Ray grabbed a lantern while Skinny loaded his gun with fresh ammunition. They made their way into the tunnel. As their eyes adjusted to the dark, they could make out cave paintings, the images eerie in the flickering lantern light.

CAW!

Out of nowhere came the sound of a crow. Skinny spun on his heel, firing blindly. The flash from the gun illuminated the mine for just a moment. But in that moment, Skinny saw the black feathers of a bird—and then the flash of a knife. Behind him, Ray had only a second to register a pair of eyes behind a mask before a shovel swung out of the dark, knocking him out.

Once more, the mine fell dark as the Lone Ranger and Tonto shared a smile. Three down. Just a few more to go. . . .

✪ ✪ ✪

"Ray? Skinny?" Cavendish called out. The mine had been quiet for too long. Walking up to the main shaft, the outlaw leaned forward and peered into the darkness. Nothing. He drew his gun and fired several rounds. But the only thing he heard was the echo of the shots on the rock walls.

Suddenly, he heard the sound of metal on metal—squeak . . . squeak . . . squeak—and then a mining cart appeared, its wheels slowly turning on the metal tracks. Cavendish and his men opened fire. In front of them, the metal cart rocked as bullets riddled its side. Still, it kept coming. And the men kept firing until the cart finally came to a stop—right in front of them.

Cavendish held up a hand. The men stopped firing. They waited to see if anyone or anything would peer out of the cart, but when nothing happened, the men made their way closer. As Cavendish peered over the side, his eyes grew wide. There, sitting just like a passenger in a train car, was a vial of nitrate! And attached to it was a burning fuse!

KA-BOOM!

The nitrate exploded, sending metal, dirt, rock, and silver flying everywhere. The men went flying, too. Cavendish was hurled a dozen feet back.

When the smoke cleared, Butch Cavendish lay on the ground, blood coming from his ears. Looking up, he saw two silhouettes appear through the dust. Butch couldn't believe his eyes. "Can't be," he said as he made out the glint of a silver star. There really were ghosts in the mine!

And then one of the ghosts spoke. "Where are they?"

"You're dead," Cavendish said in disbelief.

Reaching down, the man grabbed Cavendish by the collar. "If you hurt them, I swear to God I'll make you pay!"

As the man's face came out of the shadows, Cavendish could make out the mask. Slowly, realization dawned. "'To the full extent of the law,'" he said. "I'll be damned. The lawyer and the crazy Indian."

The Lone Ranger cocked his pistol and held it to Cavendish's head. "Tell me!"

Cavendish slowly pulled a piece of fabric from around his neck. It was Rebecca's scarf. Holding it up to his nose, he inhaled deeply. "Had a nice smell on her, didn't she?"

It was too much for the Lone Ranger to take. He began to hit Cavendish, over and over again, until he couldn't breathe anymore and his hand hurt.

When he was done, Cavendish just laughed. "You're no spirit," the outlaw said, spitting. "You're just a man in a mask. No different from me."

The Lone Ranger stared at the outlaw. Was he right? Was he as much a monster as the ugly thing in front of him? He had just wanted to save Rebecca. He had never hurt anyone in his life. And now look at him! He had blood on his hands.

Behind him, Tonto loaded a silver bullet into Cavendish's pistol. He held it out. "Now, finish him."

The Lone Ranger looked down at Cavendish, then at the blood on his hands and then at the pistol. Finally, he shook his head. "No," he said. "This isn't justice."

"The only justice is what a man takes for himself," Tonto said, once again holding out the gun.

"I can't believe that," the Lone Ranger said. "I won't."

Tonto held back a groan and said, "He cut out your brother's heart," hitting the Lone Ranger in his weak spot. "What kind of man are you?"

"I'm not a savage," the Lone Ranger said, straightening up and leveling his gaze at Tonto.

"Then I'll do it myself," Tonto said, knocking the Lone Ranger to the ground. He took a step forward, cocking the pistol as he moved. The Lone Ranger grabbed his leg, but Tonto shook him off. "You kept me from fulfilling my destiny once before. It will not happen again. The Windigo dies." He raised the gun. His arm was steady as he stared down the barrel. He had waited so very long for this moment.

Behind him, the Lone Ranger watched, his eyes full of sadness. Chief Big Bear's story flashed through his mind. The young boy driven mad. "There's no such thing as a Windigo," he said softly. "You made it up. Like you make everything up. You sold out your whole village . . . for a watch." On the ground, Cavendish looked up, his eyes narrowing on Tonto.

The Lone Ranger went on, each word stabbing into Tonto like a knife. "You're an outcast, a band apart. A messed-up kid who couldn't live with what you did." He paused, ripping off his mask and throwing it to the ground. "And there's no such thing as Windigo. Or cursed silver. Or a Spirit Walker, for that matter. I am not like you. I have a tribe."

"You have nothing," Tonto said, looking sadly at the mask lying in the dirt at his feet. "Just like me. Only you are too blind to see."

"You're wrong," the Lone Ranger replied.

Tonto's face hardened. "Then go back to your tribe. I don't need you anymore." Turning back to Cavendish, he stared at him, his eyes filled with hate. "Now, the Windigo dies."

He raised the gun. His finger began to pull back on the trigger. A moment more and he would be free of the guilt he had felt for all these years. Free to return . . .

SMACK!

Tonto slumped to the ground as behind him the Lone Ranger put the shovel back on the ground. Moving past Tonto's prone body, the Lone Ranger quickly bound Cavendish's hands.

It was done. The outlaw was in custody and Tonto had not killed him. It was exactly as the Lone Ranger wanted. But if it was what he wanted, why did he feel so bad?

✪ ✪ ✪

Rebecca Reid tossed and turned, her dreams full of nightmarish images. Her husband, lying alone in the desert. Cavendish, a cruel smile on his burned face. There was the farm, its building in ashes, and Pilar and Joe, struggling on the ground. With a gasp, she forced her eyes open. As the nightmare faded, Rebecca looked around her surroundings. She was in an opulent sleeping car. Yet the train was not moving. Outside, she could just make out a bridge. Beside her sat Kai, the Chinese woman from the Colby market.

"Where am I?" Rebecca asked, her voice weak from disuse.

Kai held out a glass of water. "Drink," she said. "Feel better." She brought the glass to Rebecca's lips and the woman sipped. A moment later her eyes fluttered closed again as the morphine in the water seeped into her system. Kai nodded. It was just as *he* wanted. . . .

CHAPTER 14

Inside the dining car of the Constitution, Danny Reid, dressed in a small suit and tie, sat in front of a miniature train set. He eagerly watched the toy zoom around curves and through fake tunnels.

Behind him, Latham Cole stood talking to his assistant, Wendell, and Captain Fuller. A map of the planned railroad route dominated one wall.

"By crossing the river," Cole said, "we will divide the Comanche and be in Promontory Summit ahead of schedule." He smiled, pleased with himself.

Fuller returned the smile. "You're a credit to the Union, Mr. Cole. And believe me, what they did to the settlements, we've given back tenfold. Comanche lack a certain purity of intention. You should see how they live." He shuddered.

Just then, there was a clatter as the toy train spun off its tracks. Reaching down, Cole picked up one of the cars. "I told you, Danny, ease off in the corners, press down on the straightaways."

"Yes, sir," Danny said, embarrassed.

Smiling reassuringly, Cole gestured. "Come over here a minute. I want to show you something." Danny stood up and followed Cole to the large map on the wall. A jagged line bisected the United States, dividing it virtually in half. Danny looked at the map, entranced, as Cole began to speak. "Since the time of Alexander the Great, man has traveled no faster than a horse could carry him. Until now. Imagine, time and space under the mastery of man. A continent connected by iron rail. Three thousand miles in less than a week. Fuel for our cities, metals for our factories, food for the masses." He held up the toy locomotive and admired it for a moment. Then he went on. "Whoever controls that, controls the future. Power that will make emperors and kings look like fools." He handed the toy back to Danny.

"You mean it's mine?" Danny asked, looking at the toy in his hand.

Cole smiled warmly. "Could be, son," he said, his eyes returning to the map. "Could be all yours."

A sound in the doorway caused Cole to look over. His eyes brightened. Rebecca stood there, beautiful as always, though her eyes were a bit glazed. She scanned the car, looking first at her son, then at Cole, and finally at Fuller. "Who are you?" she asked.

Cole introduced Captain Fuller, who nodded in greeting. "Consider yourself lucky, Mrs. Reid," Fuller said. "Had Mr. Cole not come along when he did, who knows what those outlaws might have done."

Rebecca cocked her head. It was Cole who had shot Collins? It was all so vague. She remembered being dragged out to the hill. And running. And then falling and fearing the worst. But there was a gun and Collins was dead and then . . . and then she woke up here. "We're indebted to you," she said softly.

"It is I who's indebted," Cole said, moving toward her. "Since the war I prayed God would see fit to give me a family to care for. Now he has."

As Cole spoke, Rebecca's memory began to come back stronger. "There's one left," she said.

"I'm sorry?" Cole said, confused. He had just practically told the woman he would marry her and she was talking gibberish. Then she spoke again and Cole felt his heart stop.

"A ranger still alive," Rebecca said.

"I'm afraid you're mistaken," Captain Fuller interjected.

"My men found seven graves. Perhaps when you hit your head . . ."

Gathering himself, Cole held up a hand. "If there is a ranger alive, we will scour the country until we find him. I promise you that."

Just then, the door opened again and a waiter entered, pushing a trolley of food. Eager to put the ranger subject to rest, Cole pulled out a chair for Rebecca. "Now, you should eat something," he said.

Taking his own seat, he bowed his head to pray. But what he prayed for was not the meal. He prayed that he would find that ranger before the man could tell anyone what he had seen, or what he knew.

✪ ✪ ✪

Unfortunately for Cole, the Lone Ranger was not far away. In fact, he was right outside. After leaving the Sleeping Man mine and Tonto behind, he had made his way across the desert and back toward Colby. He dragged Cavendish behind him, unbothered by the man's groans and curses. All the Lone Ranger cared about was getting back to town and bringing this man to justice. When he reached the trestle bridge outside the town, he breathed a sigh of relief and spurred his horse on.

Reaching the end of the bridge, he saw the Constitution

parked, ready to cross as soon as the construction was complete. Lights were on in several of the cars. The Lone Ranger approached. "Latham Cole!" he called out.

Inside the car, Rebecca's heart began to pound. She knew that voice! Danny seemed to think so, too, and rushed to the window, pressing his face against the glass. "Daddy!" he cried.

Rebecca stood up and made her way to the door. She started to turn the knob when Cole's hand closed around her arm. "We don't know who's out there," he said, his grip tightening.

"I intend to find out," she said stubbornly.

Without releasing her arm, Cole took a pistol out of his jacket. "Wendell," he called over his shoulder. The assistant shuffled over. "Escort Mrs. Reid and her son to the supply car. Make sure they stay there. For their own safety."

As Wendell dragged the struggling mother and son away, Cole cocked his pistol. He was so close to having everything he ever wanted. No man, no ranger, no ghost was going to take that away from him. Opening the door, he and Fuller stepped out into the night.

In front of them, a man sat on a huge white horse, a white hat hiding his face.

"What is it, friend?" Cole said, his tone insincere.

The man looked up. Seeing John Reid's face, Cole

narrowed his eyes. That was not what he had been expecting.

"This is the man you're looking for," the Lone Ranger said. With a flick of his blade, the Lone Ranger cut the rope free from his saddle. Then he yanked Cavendish forward.

Cole looked the outlaw up and down, his expression unreadable. The man returned his gaze, unflinching. "Butch Cavendish," he said. "Just like one of those great lizards buried in the desert. Last of a dying breed." Holding his gaze, he punched the man hard in the stomach. The outlaw dropped to the ground and Cole kicked him.

"That's enough," the Lone Ranger said, his tone sharp. "I brought him in for justice. Not a beating."

Cole stopped and looked up. Catching his breath, he nodded. "Of course. Captain?" Fuller approached and handed Cole a pair of handcuffs. Quickly, Cole snapped them around Cavendish's wrists.

The Lone Ranger nodded. His job was done. But something tickled at the back of his mind, making him wonder. . . .

✪ ✪ ✪

Inside the dining car of the Constitution, the Lone Ranger sat at the table, greedily eating anything he could get his hands on. Taking a break, he grabbed a pitcher and chugged down the cool liquid.

"John, isn't it?" Cole said, pouring whiskey into two crystal glasses.

The Lone Ranger nodded. "My brother's dead," he stated.

"I'm sorry," Cole replied. "We feared you were all lost. There were rumors that sustained us. A lone ranger. A masked man. A ghost, some said. But here you are—flesh and blood." He handed one of the glasses to the Lone Ranger.

Wiping his hands, the Lone Ranger accepted the glass. "Civilized society has no place for a masked man."

"Of course not," Cole said. "How do I thank you for what you've done?"

The Lone Ranger looked up, his expression serious. "By stopping this war before it's too late. Comanche didn't attack the settlements, it was Cavendish. For this." He reached into his pocket and pulled out a rock of silver. He dumped it on the table.

Cole picked it up, weighing it in his palm. "Butch Cavendish. In one man, everything I hate about this country." He walked over to the map. "No sense of the greater good. No vision. Come to think of it, not unlike your brother, Dan." As he spoke, he pulled out his pocket watch. In one well-practiced move, he spun it, catching it between his forefinger and thumb. Then he snapped it shut.

The Lone Ranger's eyes grew wide as he watched him.

He knew that trick. It was the same one Tonto was always trying—and always failing—to do. The same trick that young Tonto had seen the white man do. The very same trick that had so fascinated young Tonto that he had led the man to the silver—and lost his whole tribe.

Just then, the train lurched forward. The movement caused the Lone Ranger's glass to wobble. Reaching out to steady it, he noticed lipstick on another one of the glasses. Scanning the room, he took in the toy train set.

Unaware of what the Lone Ranger had pieced together, Cole made his way over to a large armoire as he continued talking. "Men like that just can't accept what you and I know to be true. A man can't stay the same with the world evolving around him." He opened a drawer in the armoire. "But a man can't choose his brother, can he? Almost as if his brother chooses him." He eyed the pistol lying in the drawer and smiled. "You see, that's what Cavendish and I are—brothers born in the desert all that time ago." Grabbing the gun, he whipped around, aiming it at the Lone Ranger. But the Lone Ranger was no longer at the table.

Suddenly, a gun appeared at the side of Cole's head. Out of the corner of his eye, Cole saw the Lone Ranger. "And now you've come back," the Lone Ranger said, putting the last of the pieces together. Cole and Cavendish. They had been in it together all along. "Train tracks. That's what Dan found in the desert, isn't it? He knew there'd be a war and he wouldn't go along with it, so you had him killed."

Wrenching his head to the side, Cole looked at the other man. "Like I said, no vision," he sneered. There was no need to pretend anymore. "I expected more from you."

"Stop the train," the Lone Ranger ordered.

Cole laughed. "Oh, there's no stopping this train," he said, still chuckling. "I think you know that."

Grabbing the man's arms, the Lone Ranger headed toward the door. He would see about that.

CHAPTER 15

As the train continued to move along the tracks, Rebecca clung to its side. With Danny safely hidden in the supply car, she had managed to slip away from Wendell to go get help—but now she was in even more trouble. The only way to escape had been by crawling along the side of the train. And now the train was crossing the trestle bridge. Behind her the earth fell away, and with a cry she slipped. She caught herself and took several deep breaths as her heart pounded. She had to get back inside the train.

Hesitantly, she reached up and pried open a window. Using all her strength, she pulled herself up and then slipped inside the car. For a moment, she just lay on the floor, catching her breath. Then she stood up. What she saw made her gasp. Sitting there, twirling his handcuffs without a care in the world, was Butch Cavendish.

Uncoiling himself like a snake, he moved toward her. "Cole's wrong about you," he said, reaching out. She took a swing but it was no use. He simply caught her arm. "Woman like you can't be persuaded. Got to be broke. Like a horse."

Before Rebecca could move, the outlaw swung his hand across her face. With a cry, she fell to the floor. Above her, Cavendish laughed.

✪ ✪ ✪

The Constitution swayed on the tracks as the Lone Ranger moved Cole from car to car. He needed to get to the engine and stop the train. Entering the supply car, the Lone Ranger stopped short. Standing in front of him was Danny. He had a gun in his hand, pointed right at Wendell. His mother had left him with specific directions not to let Wendell out of his sight. And so far, he hadn't. But hearing the door open, he turned. His eyes grew wide and he was filled with hope as he took in the silver badge. But the hope was short-lived. Looking at the man's face, he saw it wasn't his father.

"Put the gun down," the Lone Ranger said gently.

"Where's my daddy?" Danny asked, not lowering the weapon.

"He's dead," Cole said, nodding toward the Lone Ranger. "He killed him."

Danny's face fell and tears welled up in his eyes. His finger shook on the trigger as he struggled with the news.

"Shut up!" the Lone Ranger hissed at Cole. As he turned back to Danny, his tone softened. "That's not true. Listen to me. It's your uncle John. You remember me?"

"You trust me, don't you, Danny?" Cole said.

Danny looked over, his lip trembling. He knew Cole. Cole had given him gifts and was always nice to his mother. This other man he had barely met. But he *was* his uncle. The gun shook in his hand as he looked back and forth between the two men.

"Danny?"

Turning around, he saw his mother standing at the other end of the car. Behind her was a scary-looking man with an ugly scar on his face. "Is my daddy dead?" he asked.

Rebecca raised her eyes and looked at John, searching his face. Then she looked back at her son. "Put the gun down, Danny," she said.

"IS HE?" Danny screamed. Looking in his mother's eyes, Danny saw the answer. His face crumbled and he lowered his head.

At that moment, the door burst open again, revealing Captain Fuller, his gun aimed at the Lone Ranger. Scared,

Danny dropped his weapon. Cavendish immediately picked it up. Aiming at the Lone Ranger, he waited to see what would happen. Fuller swung his head back and forth, looking first at Cole, then at Cavendish, and finally at the Lone Ranger. He aimed his gun at Cavendish. It was a three-way standoff.

"Captain, arrest these men," the Lone Ranger said after a strained moment.

"This man is a common criminal," Cole said, nodding at the Lone Ranger. "Trespassing on railroad property."

As Fuller started to swing his gun toward him, the Lone Ranger shook his head. "Comanche didn't raid the settlements," he said quickly. He pointed at Cole and Cavendish. "They staged the attack so they could violate the treaty."

"We've heard enough. Captain," Cole urged.

"You represent the United States government," the Lone Ranger went on, ignoring Cole. "You don't work for him."

"Captain!" Cole shouted.

"They started this war!" the Lone Ranger cried at the same time.

Across the room, Fuller looked confused. What was happening? If what the man in the white hat said was true . . .

"That would mean I attacked the Comanche for no reason," he said, the full weight of what that meant dawning on him.

Seeing his chance, Cole struck home. "That's right,

Captain. The slaughter of innocents. Their blood on your hands."

As Cole's words hung in the air, the Lone Ranger held his breath, waiting to see what Fuller would do next.

Finally, Fuller spoke. "These gentlemen are with the railroad," he stated, taking his gun off Cavendish and turning it on the Lone Ranger. "Question is, who are *you*?"

As Fuller stepped forward, the Lone Ranger realized that he was outgunned and outnumbered. Things had just gone from bad to worse.

CHAPTER 16

The Constitution barreled through the night, crossing the desert faster than any horse could travel. Finally, it rolled to a stop—right in front of the Sleeping Man mine.

As the cavalry stepped out of the train and fanned out, Cole, Cavendish, and Fuller made their way to one of the shafts off to the side. Inside sat eight freight cars covered with tarps. Pulling aside one of the tarps, Cavendish revealed several tons of pure silver.

The sight made Cole smile and he reached out a hand. "Out here it's just rock," he said. "Put it on a train, it's priceless."

Picking up a hunk of silver, Fuller held it up. It sparkled in his hand. "My God." He whistled. "What could you buy with all that?"

"A country, Captain," Cole answered. "A great country for which our children will thank us."

As the three men continued to talk among themselves, a line of mine workers shuffled past, their heads lowered, big hats hiding their faces. At the end one of the workers shuffled along, carrying a stuffed crow in a cage. Noticing the strange sight, one of the soldiers cocked his head. Why would a worker be carrying a stuffed bird? But then he shrugged. What did it matter? There was a lot left to do and little time to do it.

With a shout, he ordered the men to start decoupling the cars at the end of the Constitution. They would be moved to a side track, allowing the Constitution to back up into the shaft where the silver cars were waiting. When the train steamed back into Colby, no one would know that the cars had been switched.

In all the confusion, the worker carrying the birdcage slipped inside the mine and disappeared from view. But he hadn't gone completely unnoticed. Out of the corner of his eye, a soldier saw the worker and started after him.

✪ ✪ ✪

Inside the Constitution's parlor car, Rebecca watched as workers raced around, preparing the train. Then she saw the Lone Ranger pass by the window, bound and escorted by soldiers. She gulped. That could mean only one thing. He was going to be executed.

Rebecca whirled around as the door behind her opened. It was Cole. "Please don't do this," she begged, pointing outside to the Lone Ranger. "I'll do what you want."

For a moment, he didn't speak. "I was at Gettysburg," he finally said. "Twelve thousand casualties before lunch. Know what I learned in all that death?" He leaned close. When she didn't say anything, he answered his own question. "Nothing is accomplished without sacrifice."

What did this man know about sacrifice? She had already lost her husband. She was *not* going to lose John, too. Before she could stop herself, Rebecca spit in Cole's face.

Cole's cheeks went red and his eyes filled with rage. Grabbing her, he pulled back his hand, about to strike.

"Leave her alone!" Danny shouted, jumping at Cole.

Spinning around, Cole backhanded the boy, knocking him to the ground. He had been nice long enough. Now he was going to make everyone pay.

✪ ✪ ✪

Outside, the Constitution began to back up, while inside the mine, the head engineer stood in one of the freight cars. He wanted to make sure everything was ready to go when the main train and the freight cars connected. A shout next to the car made him look out. A soldier was holding a gun at one of the workers. In his hand the worker held a cage, which in turn held a black bird, though the bird did not appear to be moving. As the engineer peered closer, his eyes grew wide. Workers often kept birds in cages to detect odorless but dangerous gas, and the bird in this cage looked very dead—a clear sign that there was lethal gas in the mines. "There's gas!" the engineer shouted. "GAS!" Releasing the freight cars' breaks, he took off.

As his words echoed through the mine, people began to run. The soldier holstered his gun and ran for fresh air as the rest of the workers exited the mine, leaving the worker with the bird by himself. Slowly, the worker took off his hat and smiled. It was Tonto. Nothing cleared a mine faster. . . .

★ ★ ★

The Lone Ranger stood, blindfolded, on one of the mine's manual car platforms. A line of cavalry soldiers stood opposite him, awaiting their orders.

"Ready!" Fuller shouted.

The men gripped their rifles.

"Aim!"

In unison, seven rifles lifted into the air, their muzzles pointed right at the Lone Ranger.

"FIRE!" Just as Fuller dropped his sword, all chaos broke loose. With a loud clang, the Constitution collided with the freight cars. As the firing squad was distracted by the noise, their shots went wild, ricocheting into the air.

Behind his blindfold, the Lone Ranger narrowed his eyes. What was going on out there? And more important, how was he still alive? Suddenly, he felt a jerk as the platform began to move beneath him. Then he heard a familiar voice.

"Have no fear, Kemosabe," Tonto whispered. He stood at the front of the manual mine car, his hands poised above the pump that served as the car's engine.

"Tonto?" the Lone Ranger said, surprised. Never had he ever thought he would be so happy to hear that crazy, bird-wearing man's voice.

But before Tonto could reply, there was a low whizzing sound followed by a thunk. And then another. And another. Arrows shot out of the night sky, fired by invisible attackers. "What was that?" the Lone Ranger asked nervously.

THUNK! Another arrow shot down, hitting the pump in front of Tonto's face. He gulped. "No reason for concern," he said as he began to pump as fast as his arms would let him.

Behind them, the air filled with the sound of the Comanche war cry.

Helpless, the Lone Ranger could do nothing but wait for Tonto's orders as they moved along. All around them, soldiers fell to the ground, arrows sticking out of their chests.

Out of the corner of his eye, Tonto saw the moving train.

Whoever was driving seemed to be having trouble, and the iron giant was heading *into* the mine rather than out of it. Looking up at the engine room, Tonto saw Latham Cole. No wonder the train was going back. Cole had seen them. And he was as eager to prevent the two men from leaving as Tonto was eager to prevent Cole from taking the silver.

Tonto pumped more frantically. A moment later, they were plunged into near darkness as they entered the mine. Behind them, the Constitution got closer and closer.

"Tonto?" the Lone Ranger shouted nervously, the sound of the engine nearly deafening in the mine. "What is that?"

Glancing over his shoulder, Tonto cringed. The train was catching up—fast. He made a decision. "We jump," he called, turning back to the Lone Ranger.

For the first time since they had met, the Lone Ranger didn't balk. "Left or right?" he asked.

"We jump now!" Tonto shouted, throwing himself off the platform. He landed with a thud and began rolling down an abandoned mine shaft. A moment later, the Lone Ranger landed next to him.

On the track above, the Constitution slammed into the platform, demolishing it. Then there was a loud screech as the train came to a stop and began to reverse. As Tonto untied the Lone Ranger and removed his blindfold, they shared a smile of relief. That had been way too close.

But their relief was short-lived. Hearing the sound of something rolling, they looked up just in time to see a barrel of kerosene moving right toward them. Clearly, Cole wasn't taking any chances. He wanted the men dead—once and for all. Another barrel rolled toward them. And then there was a flash of light up on the tracks. A fuse had been lit, and soon, the rolling barrels of kerosene would explode.

This was not good.

Turning, they began to run for their lives. Looking over his shoulder, Tonto picked up the pace. Behind them was a huge fireball. Following Cole's orders, Cavendish had lit another barrel of kerosene on fire and rolled it after them. And it was rolling very, very fast.

Up ahead, the mine shaft began to narrow. But in the dimming light, Tonto spied the sparkle of water. Nodding to the Lone Ranger, they raced right at it and jumped in, ducking under the cool surface. A moment later there was a loud *BOOM*, and the water shook as the barrel exploded.

✪ ✪ ✪

Outside, the cavalry and Comanche continued their fight. But the soldiers were at a disadvantage. They were running out of ammunition and didn't know the landscape. They couldn't hide as easily and they were on foot. The Comanche knew the Sleeping Man mountain—and they had horses. It looked like they were going to win.

And then Fuller unveiled the Gatling guns.

Fuller brought down his sword and the soldiers began firing. The automatic weapons sprayed bullets furiously, cutting down anything and anyone that crossed their path. One by one, the Comanche were shot down. Red Knee fell, his body landing in the river, which had been clear but now ran red. Horses galloped by, trying to outrace the horrible weapon. And he guns kept firing.

Watching his warriors fall, Chief Big Bear turned and stared at the Gatling guns. Then he looked at Fuller. With a loud whoop, he charged—straight at the cavalry leader. But Fuller was ready for him. Grabbing the man's wrist, he drove his saber into Chief Big Bear.

Behind them, the Gatling guns fell silent. There was no one left to shoot. As smoke drifted out of the automatic weapons, Chief Big Bear's wise eyes looked right into Fuller's. There was no fear, no pain. Just understanding, as though he had known this day would come. And then, as Fuller watched, the old man sank to the ground.

Looking down at his bloodstained gloves, Fuller began to shake. What had he just done?

CHAPTER 17

Coughing and sputtering, the Lone Ranger dragged himself up onto the riverbank. Beside him, Tonto fell onto the dry land. For a moment, they just lay there, gasping for breath. Then Tonto raised himself up.

In front of them, the river was red. Tonto swallowed. It was the image that had haunted him his whole life. Overcome with emotion, he turned his back on the Lone Ranger, who looked at him with sadness. Tonto couldn't take the pity. He needed his bird. Scanning the riverbank, he found it. The creature was lying limp near the shore. Getting to his feet, Tonto went over and picked it up.

Behind him, the Lone Ranger sat silently. Finally, he stood up and joined Tonto. "You were right," the Lone Ranger said.

"There is no justice. Cole controls everything. The railroad. The cavalry. Everything. If men like him represent the law, I'd rather be an outlaw."

Tonto nodded. He had been waiting for this moment. "That's why you wear the mask," he said, reaching into his pouch. He pulled out the leather and handed it to the Lone Ranger.

Taking it, the Lone Ranger nodded. Finally, he understood. Right and wrong were not black and white. Just like good and bad weren't so clearly separated. Wearing a mask didn't make him a bad man. It made him a man with the ability to do good.

The sound of a tree branch splitting made them both look up. The Lone Ranger smiled. Standing high in the tree, wearing his hat, was the white spirit horse.

"Something very wrong with that horse," Tonto said.

The Lone Ranger nodded. That might be the case, but he didn't care. Now they had a way to get back to Colby.

✪ ✪ ✪

A celebration was in full swing at Promontory Summit. The Transcontinental Railroad was complete. On the train tracks, the Constitution's engine touched the engine of the Jupiter. One train from the West, the other from the East. The United States were now, well and truly, united. As a brass band played, men, women, and children eagerly awaited their chance to get close to the trains and put their hands on a part of history.

On a platform nearby, Vice President Colfax addressed the crowds. Behind him sat various shareholders and the governor of Texas.

"Ladies and gentlemen," Colfax said, his voice booming. "We are here today to celebrate a dream. And now, I would like to introduce the man who made that dream a reality." He gestured toward a large man sitting on the closest chair. The soft man was the embodiment of a robber baron, with his manicured mustache and gaudy clothes. "Chairman of the Transcontinental Railroad Corporation. Mr. Lewis Habberman the Third."

Slowly, the big man got to his feet and made his way to the platform. "I thank you, Mr. Vice President," Habberman began. "My family thanks you. But I can't take credit alone. The working men before you deserve your applause, as does one man in particular. A more dedicated, loyal employee the railroad could not ask for. Mr. Latham Cole!"

From the side of the platform, Cole stepped forward. He waved to the crowd, a smile plastered on his face.

"It is my honor to present you with this," Habberman continued, holding out a pocket watch. "A testament of our thanks."

Eyeing the timepiece, Cole struggled not to roll his eyes. Another pocket watch. It was infuriating. But he would get the last laugh. When he was a millionaire and richer than the fat robber baron, he would show him how much he cared for his stupid pocket watch.

⚫ ⚫ ⚫

The ceremony was over. Everyone was blissfully unaware of Latham Cole's plans for the railroad and what was held in the freight cars of the Constitution. As people meandered off to enjoy the rest of the day, Cole signaled to the dignitaries making their way off the podium.

"Mr. Habberman," he called. "If you and the other shareholders would come this way, I have a little surprise for you."

Suddenly, there was the sound of a muffled explosion. Cole cocked his head. In the distance, he could just make out a small plume of smoke rising.

"What was that?" Habberman asked, his chins jiggling nervously.

Cole waved a hand. "Tunneling for the supply routes," he said calmly. "No reason for concern. This way, please." Turning, he began to lead the men into the small station house. Cavendish, dressed in fancy new clothes that did nothing to hide his ugly scars, fell into step beside him. "Get the girl," Cole instructed out of the corner of his mouth. Then, plastering on a smile, he entered the station house, concerned about the explosion in the distance.

✪ ✪ ✪

INTERLUDE—San Francisco

"Where'd you get the explosives?" Will asked. He had been listening to every word—confusing and otherwise—that the elderly Tonto had spoken. But he didn't remember anything about getting explosives.

Tonto popped his head out of the fake teepee. "I told you," he said.

"No, you didn't," Will replied, shaking his head. Tonto had told him about a talking horse, a mountain that looked like a man, a huge battle, to name just a few. But nowhere in all that had he mentioned the explosives. Will shook his head again and crossed his arms over his chest, waiting.

Tonto emerged from the teepee. In his hand he held a hanger on which hung a black suit and a bowler hat. "We had a plan," he said, brushing off the suit with a broken badminton racquet. Will narrowed his eyes. Where had he gotten that? Tonto went on. "It was a good plan."

He continued brushing off the suit, his eyes fading as he

thought back to that day long before. Then he spoke, filling Will in.

The day they had robbed the Colby Municipal Bank, they hadn't been after the gold or cash kept in its vault. They had been after Cole's nitrate. The railroad man had ordered his assistant to put it somewhere safe. And Wendell, lacking in imagination, had figured the safest place was, well, a safe. He had carefully stored away the explosives so they would be ready when Cole needed them. What he hadn't counted on was the Lone Ranger. The masked man had figured out Cole's hiding spot. Then it was only a matter of a little heist and they were in control of enough nitrate to blow up a small town.

As Tonto spoke, Will smiled. He knew it! The Lone Ranger would never have really robbed a bank. But then, what was he going to do with all that nitrate?

CHAPTER 18

Inside the Constitution's parlor car, Rebecca stood silently, her face pressed up against the window. She had heard the explosion and seen the smoke, and she had a pretty good idea of what it meant.

The door behind her creaked open and Cavendish entered, two soldiers flanking him. "He's coming for you," Rebecca said. "Just like Frank said."

Cavendish took a step closer. "What you got that makes them Reid boys so hot under the collar, anyway?" he said. He leaned in menacingly. "Maybe I'll find out."

Rebecca stared at the man's ugly face. It no longer frightened her. She simply felt repulsion. "You're going to die today." A flicker of something flashed across his face and

Rebecca smiled. He was the one who was scared now. "If I'm not there to watch, you think of me."

With a cry of rage, Cavendish lunged at Rebecca. Grabbing her, he began to shake her roughly.

"Leave her alone!" Danny cried, stepping out of the shadows where he'd been hiding.

Cavendish released Rebecca but kept one hand tight on her arm. "Mr. Cole wants a word with your mama," he sneered. Locking eyes with Rebecca, he added, "Give me any trouble, you'll never see your boy again."

The woman nodded. She wouldn't give him any trouble, sure. But she had a feeling trouble was already on its way.

And she was right. Outside the train, Captain Fuller and his men were doing a final check to make sure no unwanted visitors would be taking the journey west. Noticing several soldiers loafing beside the covered freight cars, Fuller marched over.

"You check under the carriage?" he asked. The men nodded. "Well, check again."

The men grumbled and got to their feet. They had checked. More than once. What was the captain so nervous about? Who would even think about hiding under the train?

But what they didn't know was that at that very moment someone *was* hiding under the train. Tonto, his fingers gripping the train tightly, held his breath as he heard the cavalry begin their inspection. He had nowhere to go. If they found him . . .

Suddenly, he heard a commotion. Looking over, he saw the bottoms of several women's dresses. And one very white fake leg. He smiled and waited to hear what would happen.

Fuller had also seen the dresses—and the women in them. Leading the group was the woman with bright red hair. "May I help you, madam?" he asked, blocking them from coming closer.

Red Harrington smiled. Then she lifted her fake leg onto a stack of crates. "Seems I have a run in my stocking," she replied, all sugar and spice. Raising her skirt, she displayed the white limb.

Fuller's eyes grew wide and he involuntarily took a step closer. "Ivory?" he asked, stretching out a hand as if to touch it.

Red smiled. Every man had his thing. "Most mistake it for scrimshaw," she answered.

"Heathens," Fuller said under his breath, forgetting all about his duties and the train that still needed to be checked. The other soldiers were equally distracted by Red's girls.

Under the train, Tonto nodded and resumed making his way down the car's length. He would have to remember to thank Red—if he ever got out of this adventure alive.

Back at the station house, the railroad's shareholders entered a long, narrow room. A big rectangular table dominated the room. In front of each chair a legal document had been placed.

"Have a seat," Cole instructed. Confused, everyone did as they were told. "The men in this room represent the finest families in this country as well as the controlling interest in the Transcontinental Railroad Corporation." Cole began to pace the room, his voice becoming more animated as he moved. At the table, the shareholders raised their glasses. Cole went on. "I congratulate you. Through money you inherited you are now in a position to control what I built with my hands, my sweat, my blood."

Slowly, the shareholders lowered their glasses.

Pleased, Cole continued his speech. "What you cannot know is that over the last six months I have leveraged a position that will make me the single largest shareholder when the company is listed Monday morning on the New York City Stock Exchange." He paused, savoring the moment. "In essence, gentlemen, you work for me."

Around the table, the shareholders exchanged looks.

What was going on? Could this be true? "You propose to *buy* the railroad?" one of them asked.

"Just the majority stake," Cole replied, nodding.

"Do you have any idea the cost?" another shareholder ventured.

Stepping forward from where he had been hovering, Wendell held up a slip of paper. "Fifty-eight point two million dollars," he said matter-of-factly.

"Each of those freight cars contains four and a half tons of purest raw silver," Cole went on, nodding toward the Constitution. "Once it reaches the bank in San Francisco, sixty-five million dollars' worth. What you might call a hostile takeover." Reaching into his pocket, he pulled out Habberman's token. "You can keep the watch." Throwing it on the table, he smiled as the shareholders began to shout among themselves. It was the sweetest sound he had ever heard.

✪ ✪ ✪

Outside the station house, the Lone Ranger and Tonto were busy putting their plan into motion. Crawling under the train, Tonto stopped beneath the parlor car. Looking up through a grate in the floor, he saw Danny Reid. Wrapping his fingers around the grate, he pulled himself up until his painted face was pressed to the brass. Danny, who had been acting as errand boy for the soldiers guarding him, saw the fingers and then Tonto's face. His eyes grew wide.

Holding a finger to his lips, Tonto motioned for Danny to come closer. Making sure the soldiers weren't looking, Danny leaned down, pretending to have dropped a piece of fruit. Tonto nodded and then pushed a single silver bullet through the grate. Danny grabbed it and pocketed the ammunition.

That part of the plan complete, Tonto continued on his way, but not before snagging a grape from Danny. After all, he was hungry.

At the stable, Red's bodyguard, Homer, was doing his part to help. All the cavalry's horses were inside, being guarded by several of the soldiers. Eyeing the men, Homer drove his wagon up to the stable entrance. In the back of the wagon, several crates marked PICKLES rattled about.

"Hey, you can't leave that here," one of the soldiers shouted.

Homer shrugged his big shoulders. "Mr. Cole's pickles," he said. "Take it up with him." He jumped down off the wagon and walked away, leaving the pickles behind.

While Red continued to distract Fuller and his men, Tonto finally arrived at the Constitution's engine. Inside, the engineer and firemen sat entranced by the festivities going on outside. They were completely unaware of Tonto as he climbed up into the car, his knife drawn. He took a step forward, his shoe scraping on the floor.

Hearing the noise, the engineer whirled around. His eyes grew wide as he took in Tonto. "What do you think you're doing?"

"Robbery," Tonto replied.

The engineer laughed. "We don't have no money, boy," he said, chuckling.

Tonto held up his blade and the man instantly stopped laughing. "Train robbery," he corrected.

Exchanging looks, the engineer and the firemen hastily climbed out of the car.

Turning to the train's controls, Tonto eyed them curiously. There was one small hiccup in their plan. He had no idea how to drive a train. But how hard could it be? Randomly, he began to pull on various levers. With a groan, the train lurched forward.

Tonto smiled. That hadn't been so hard after all. He pulled another series of levers and the train began to move backward. His smile faded. So maybe he still had a few things to figure out.

CHAPTER 19

Back in the station house, the shareholders were still in an uproar. Just as their voices reached a fever pitch, the door to the room opened and Cavendish entered, pushing Rebecca ahead of them. The shareholders barely noticed.

"This is an outrage!" one of the men cried.

"I, for one, am not going to sit here and negotiate with one of my *employees*," Habberman said, struggling to his feet. Lifting his head, his eyes grew wide. Cole had a gun in his hand. It was pointed right at him.

"Then let's get down to it, shall we?" he asked. He pulled the trigger. Habberman let out a scream as he fell to the floor, clutching his leg. "Gentlemen," he went on. "Due to an accident, your chairman has had to take a sudden leave of absence. You'll need a replacement. Nominations?" He looked around the room, the gun at his side still smoking.

For a moment, no one spoke. Finally, one of the men held up his shaking hand. "I nominate Mr. Latham Cole," he said.

"I second," another one added.

Turning to look at Rebecca, Cole smiled, as if to say, *I told you so*. Then, turning back to the shareholders, he nodded. "I accept."

Behind him, there was a commotion. But Cole didn't bother to turn around. This was the best moment of his life. He controlled the railway. And in a few days more, he would be one of the richest men in America. Nothing could go wrong now.

"Um, Mr. Cole," Wendell stammered, pointing out the window.

Cole stifled a groan. What did the man want? Could he not just have a moment to enjoy his victory? Turning, he followed Wendell's finger. He felt his heart stop for a beat and then begin pounding wildly. Outside, in front of his very eyes, the Constitution was moving. The big iron machine pulled back from the Jupiter, destroying the iconic moment when the trains had made history. It knocked over the stage, ripped down bunting, and sent people running as it moved farther along the track. "They're stealing my train," he hissed in disbelief.

"They're *stealing* your *silver*," a shareholder corrected him. "No silver, no deal."

With a cry of rage, Cole raced out of the room. Cavendish, Wendell, and Rebecca followed close behind.

Outside, they were met with chaos. A loud explosion rocked the air as, nearby, the stable entrance blew up, trapping the horses inside. Now the cavalry had no way to follow the train.

There was another bang, and Cole turned to see Fuller fall back away from Red, the woman's leg still smoking from where she had shot at the wagon, blowing it up in a spectacular explosion. It hadn't been full of pickles after all.

Cole felt a wave of hot anger wash over him. Everything he had worked so hard for, everything he had schemed for and plotted for, was being destroyed right before his eyes.

Just then, the engine car passed right in front of Cole. Sitting at the driver's seat, looking happy as a pig in mud, was Tonto. With a tip of his head, he blew the train's horn as it continued reversing through town.

"Shoot him!" Cole yelled, turning to one of the soldiers standing nearby. The young lad was manning one of the Gatling guns. He hesitated.

"Danny's in there!" Rebecca shouted, struggling in Cavendish's grip.

Cole ignored her. "That's an ORDER!" he screamed to the soldier.

RATATATATATATATAT!

The air filled with the sound of gunfire. As people ran screaming, bullets ricocheted off the Constitution, ripping holes in its side and shattering windows. From inside the parlor car, soldiers clambered out onto the train's roof. Seeing his men on board, Fuller ran up and jumped on the train, soldiers following. Soon they had joined the men on the Constitution's roof.

Suddenly, a single white lariat flew through the air, hooking around the Gatling gun. Turning, Rebecca gasped. Up on the roof of the courthouse, the Lone Ranger reared back on his big white horse. He gave the lariat one swift tug. It tightened around the Gatling gun and then, as Rebecca watched, the gun began to swivel. In moments, it was firing right at the soldiers on top of the train!

The Lone Ranger continued to pull on the lariat as soldiers ducked for cover atop the Constitution. The Gatling gun swiveled farther and farther, bullets flying. Finally, with one last tug, the Lone Ranger disengaged the gun. It fell silent.

Looking around, the Lone Ranger started to smile,

pleased to see no one had been hurt. But the smile faded on his lips. Cole had ordered his men to start the Jupiter's engine. The other train was already in motion, and as the Lone Ranger watched, Cole dragged Rebecca inside. He had to do something—fast!

"YA!" Kicking his horse forward, the Lone Ranger began to gallop along the rooftops, gaining on the departing trains. He looked over his shoulder, gauging the distance between the roof and the iron beast. He gulped. It wasn't exactly close. But he was running out of rooftop! Taking a deep breath, he tugged on the reins and gave the white horse a mighty kick. The horse leaped, flying through the air. They hovered for a moment, the Lone Ranger's heart in his throat. And then with a clatter of hooves on steel, they landed on the Jupiter's roof. A moment later, they passed the last building. The Lone Ranger let out a sigh of relief. That had been a little too close for comfort.

As the two trains hurtled into the desert, the Lone Ranger lowered his hat. It was time to go save Rebecca. And bring justice to Cole and Cavendish once and for all.

✪ ✪ ✪

The Constitution flew backward along the track, Tonto at the engine. Looking out the window, he saw the Jupiter, which was moving forward and gaining speed. Cole stood in the Jupiter's engine car, pushing her on faster and faster, while Cavendish lowered himself onto a wooden platform of the train so he could get a better shot at Tonto. It wouldn't be long before the two trains would once again be touching. Tonto couldn't let that happen.

He pushed the throttle down as far as it would go. But they were already at maximum speed. And all the silver was slowing them down. He had to think of something—and soon—or else the Jupiter would run right into the Constitution!

Glancing ahead, Tonto smiled. A switch was rapidly approaching. If Tonto could hit it in time, the Jupiter would jump to the track running parallel to his. It would hopefully buy him some time. But he needed something to hit the switch. He scanned the small engine room, his eyes coming to rest on a shovel. Picking it up, he moved closer to the car's door.

The switch came closer. And closer. And still closer. At the very last moment, Tonto held out the shovel. *CLANG!* It hit the switch and the tracks instantly began to split. With a mighty iron groan, the Jupiter tilted on its wheels as it followed the track that veered slightly right. The Constitution continued on straight.

Stepping back into the engine room, Tonto smiled to himself. That had gone rather well, or so he thought. As

As Tonto looked up, his smile faded. The Jupiter, which was moving faster without the weight of the silver, was now right next to the Constitution. Which meant everyone, including Cole, had a much better shot at Tonto. He was a sitting duck. As gunshots once more filled the air, Tonto returned fire with whatever was handy. He tossed a bucket, some coal, even a shoe as he frantically tried to think of a new plan.

Suddenly, he knew just what to do. Turning back to the controls, he reached out and yanked—hard—on the brake lever.

The air filled with a horrible screeching, and sparks flew as the Constitution began to come to a stop. On the parallel track, the Jupiter flew past. As Tonto watched it go, his eyes grew wide. On the roof of the other train, the Lone Ranger and his horse were racing along. How had they gotten there? Then he shook his head. Nature was indeed out of balance. But for once, that was okay with him.

Captain Fuller was furious. He had let the train be stolen right out from underneath his nose all because of a pretty lady with a fake leg. He was determined to fix things. And that meant getting the silver back. Fuller made his way down to the head of the freight cars. Frantically, he began to try to decouple the cars. But the speed of the train was making it hard and he let out a frustrated groan as he failed over and over again.

Hearing a strange noise, he looked up. He watched as the masked man raced across the Jupiter, riding a white horse. Leaning out, Fuller called to Cole. "The ranger!" Fuller shouted. "He's on the roof!"

Inside the Jupiter's engine, Cole hovered over the controls. On the floor nearby, Rebecca sat, cradling her head in her arms. Hearing Fuller's shout, Cole craned his neck out the window. He stepped back, his face murderous. "How many times do I have to tell you to kill that ranger?" he screamed to Cavendish as the other men entered the engine cab.

Cavendish followed the other man's gaze. "Just once," the outlaw said. Walking over, he grabbed Rebecca and yanked her to her feet. She would come in handy.

Quickly, the outlaw made his way out onto the roof. Using Rebecca as a shield, he glanced around until he spotted the Lone Ranger. He began to fire.

Back on the Constitution, Fuller resumed working on the coupling. He tugged and shook the pin holding the freight cars to the Constitution. Grabbing the pin one last time, he heaved with all his strength. To his amazement, the pin finally slid free. The silver was no longer attached to the Constitution. But instead of slowing down, the freed freight cars kept coming.

★ ★ ★

Up on the roof of the Jupiter, the Lone Ranger dodged and weaved as Cavendish continued to pepper him with gunfire from several cars away. Out of the corner of his eye, he saw the Constitution. Suddenly, it appeared to rise higher. That was strange. As the Lone Ranger looked ahead, his eyes grew wide. The Constitution wasn't getting higher. The Jupiter was getting lower! They were heading right into a tunnel. And on horseback, he would never clear it.

Noticing the ranger's look, Cavendish turned. The tunnel was now just a hundred feet away—and coming up fast. Throwing Rebecca down, Cavendish followed suit, pressing his body as close to the roof of the train as possible. On his car, the Lone Ranger kicked his horse forward— racing toward the oncoming tunnel. Seventy-five feet. Fifty feet. The Lone Ranger kept spurring his horse faster. Peering up, Rebecca let out a shout. He was never going to make it. Twenty-five feet. Ten feet. Five feet. Just as the car plummeted into the tunnel, the Lone Ranger and his horse jumped down into a flatbed car, the roof of the tunnel passing harmlessly above.

The Lone Ranger let out his breath and reached down to

pat his horse. That had been a close one. Spurring the horse on, the Lone Ranger opened the train's door and made his way inside a passenger car. Several of the passengers, unaware of the chaos happening around them, screamed. The Lone Ranger moved along, apologizing as he went.

Entering the next car, he was about to apologize some more when the windows shattered. Looking over, the Lone Ranger saw Captain Fuller, keeping pace in the parallel train. He had a gun in each hand and was firing. The Lone Ranger ducked down on the side of his horse. They made their way to the end of the car—and then the gunfire stopped. Looking over at the other train to see what had happened, the ranger smiled. Tonto stood, shovel in hand and Fuller at his feet, knocked out cold.

The Lone Ranger nodded his thanks. Now that that was taken care of, he needed to find Cavendish.

CHAPTER 20

As the freed silver cars continued to barrel along behind the Constitution, the Lone Ranger quietly made his way onto the roof of the Jupiter's freight car. Ahead of him, his back turned, stood Butch Cavendish. He held on tightly to Rebecca.

The Lone Ranger straightened up and called out the outlaw's name. Whirling around, Cavendish fired his gun. *Click.* He pulled again. *Click.* The gun was empty. Seeing her chance, Rebecca tried to break away. But Cavendish pulled her back.

"Let her go," the Lone Ranger said, his tone threatening.

"Gladly," Cavendish said, shoving her closer to the edge of the speeding train. "Unless you want to put that gun down."

The Lone Ranger's jaw hardened and his face remained unreadable. "Go ahead," he replied, nodding at Rebecca. "She married Dan, not me."

"John!" Rebecca shouted. She stared at him, her eyes questioning. He couldn't possibly mean it, could he?

Cavendish seemed to think so. With a shrug, he gave her one last shove. She let out an ear-piercing scream as she fell over the side . . . only to land on the back of the big white horse.

Above, Cavendish was unaware that his attempt at hurting the Lone Ranger hadn't worked. With the girl out of the way, he was eager to put an end to the Lone Ranger and his stupid mask once and for all.

The Lone Ranger raised his gun.

"What are you going to do, counselor?" Cavendish said, letting out a laugh. "Shoot me?"

"That's right," the Lone Ranger replied, pulling the trigger.

Click. It was empty.

Gulping, the Lone Ranger took a step back as Cavendish pulled out his knife. The Lone Ranger raised his fists.

"Don't tell me. You boxed in law school?" Cavendish said.

He started to laugh, again but then, out of the corner of his eye, he saw a ladder rise from the Constitution. On top of it was Tonto. Taking advantage of the outlaw's distraction, the Lone Ranger reached out and punched him square in the face. The outlaw buckled and collapsed in a heap.

Confident that Cavendish couldn't cause any more trouble, the Lone Ranger helped Tonto off the swinging ladder, and then together they made their way down to the coupling that connected the passenger cars to the Jupiter's engine. They needed to get the passengers safe.

"Where's the girl?" Tonto asked as the Lone Ranger began fiddling with the pin.

"Where's the silver?" he replied, not bothering to look up.

Tonto raised an eyebrow. That was a very good question.

✪ ✪ ✪

Leaving the Lone Ranger to work on the coupling, Tonto raced back onto the roof of the Jupiter to take stock of the situation. It wasn't good. While he could see the silver rocketing along on its own track behind the Constitution, he could also make out a bridge that was clearly still under construction. And from the looks of it, the Jupiter was going to go right over the bridge, while the runaway silver would follow its tracks under the bridge.

Breaking into a sprint, Tonto raced along the roof of the Jupiter. Then he threw himself into the air. The wind whistled in his ears as he soared between the two trains and then, with a thud, landed on the last silver car, his legs dangling over the edge. He hung there for a moment before pulling himself safely onto the roof. Staggering to his feet, he began to make his way along the silver cars. Up ahead, he could see that the two tracks were about to converge once more. He gulped.

Unaware of the pending collision, the Lone Ranger pulled the coupling pin free. There was a groan and then the passenger cars pulled away. Now there were five trains running along the two tracks—the Constitution's passenger cars and the Jupiter freight cars on one; the silver cars, the Constitution's engine, and the Jupiter's caboose and passenger cars on the other. Standing up, the Lone Ranger turned to go help his friend when he heard the distinct click of a gun barrel. He slowly turned around. Behind him stood Cavendish, now back on his feet and with his reloaded gun in hand.

"This time," Cavendish said, smiling evilly, "you stay dead."

Just then, the two tracks came perilously close, and the silver cars clipped the sides of the Jupiter's remaining freight cars. There was an ear-piercing screech as metal scratched along metal. Thrown off balance, Cavendish fired his gun wildly as the car began to pitch sideways.

Struggling to keep his footing, the Lone Ranger whirled his lariat in the air. Then he threw it, the end looping around a passing tree. As he was flung into the air, the Jupiter's engine turned completely sideways and began sliding along the track. Behind it, the Constitution barreled along backward, heading straight at the crippled Jupiter. From the doorway of the Jupiter, Cavendish looked up just in time to see Captain Fuller. The man stood at the end of the other train, the distinct imprint of a shovel on his face. As the two men locked eyes, they both knew it was too late.

A moment later, the Constitution's passenger cars slammed into the Jupiter's freight cars. There was a huge explosion of pulverized wood and metal, and then a giant ball of fire burst into the sky.

The Lone Ranger watched it all unfold as he flew through the air. Out of the corner of his eye he saw a flash of white. He let go of the lariat and fell, landing face-to-face with Rebecca, who was still riding the big white horse. He smiled. "Wrong brother?" he asked.

SLAP! Reaching out, Rebecca hit him across the face. "Not today," she said, pulling him in for a deep kiss.

His cheek still stinging, the Lone Ranger kissed her right back. That day he most certainly was the right brother.

✪ ✪ ✪

Inside the engine car of the Jupiter, Latham Cole had not given up on getting his silver. While he had lost Cavendish, the bridge had proved invaluable, because it had put him back on the same track as the silver. In fact, the freight cars were just behind him—and gaining fast.

With a thud, the silver car and the engine collided. Cole smiled. Now he just needed to make sure he'd gotten rid of that pesky Comanche and that annoying Lone Ranger.

The annoying Lone Ranger was, at that very moment, racing alongside what remained of the Jupiter. Getting his horse as close as possible to the big iron giant, he helped Rebecca swing onto the train. Making sure she and Danny were safe, he spurred his horse on. He needed to get to Cole.

It didn't take him long to find the man. Unfortunately, when he did, he saw that Cole had a gun pointed right at Tonto. The impact of the Jupiter's hooking up to the silver cars had thrown Tonto to the ground. Now he lay on the roof of the silver car, unable to escape.

"Time's up," the Lone Ranger heard Cole say.

He reached for his gun and flipped it open. Empty. How could he save Tonto now?

"Uncle John!"

Looking beside him, the Lone Ranger saw Danny leaning out a window. He was holding something shiny in his hand. It was the silver bullet! The Lone Ranger reached out his hand and Danny threw the bullet. Grabbing it, the Lone Ranger quickly loaded his gun.

The Lone Ranger raised his arm. It was a hard angle under normal circumstances. But now, while riding a galloping horse and aiming at a man on a speeding train? It was nearly impossible.

"I'm a Spirit Walker," the Lone Ranger said. Then he closed his eyes. "I can't miss."

He fired.

The bullet whizzed through the air, hitting Cole's gun. The weapon flew from his hand just as the Constitution's engine slammed into the back of the silver cars. Now it was a giant two-headed iron horse. Racing into the engine cab of the Constitution, Rebecca and Danny slammed on the brakes. As sparks flew, the two trains engaged in a heavy metal tug-of-war, the silver cars stuck in the middle.

On top of the silver car, Tonto got to his feet. Picking up Cole's gun, he aimed it at his head. "All these years, I thought you were Windigo," he said sadly. "But you are just a man."

Cole cocked his head. "Who are you?" he replied.

Tonto reached into his pocket and pulled out the watch. He tossed it at Cole. "Bad trade," he said.

Cole looked down at the watch and then at Tonto, realization finally dawning. Before he could say another word, though, Tonto fired the gun at the coupling below. Stepping back onto the braking Constitution, he watched as the Jupiter sped ahead, a helpless Cole on board. . . .

INTERLUDE—San Francisco

"You let him get away!" Will shouted, outraged.

That was how the story ended? With the bad guy not getting justice? That wasn't what was supposed to happen!

"No," Tonto said, shaking his head. He had changed into the black suit and was now adjusting his hat in a handheld mirror.

Watching him, Will narrowed his eyes. What did he mean no? And then, he remembered. "The bridge!" he said, growing excited.

"What bridge?" Tonto asked, feigning ignorance. But Tonto knew exactly what bridge Will was talking about.

The image was imprinted in his brain. And as he told Will what had happened, it was as though it were happening all over again. . . .

As Tonto had watched, the train carrying Latham Cole, his old pocket watch, and four and a half tons of silver had plummeted from the broken bridge. It fell down, down, down, crashing into the roaring river below. A moment later, the Constitution had screeched to a stop, the final car dangling over the river.

Leaning over to get a better look, Tonto lost his balance and almost fell into the ravine. But the Lone Ranger's hand reached out and grabbed him just in the nick of time. The man had saved him. Not for the first time, and certainly not for the last.

Together, they looked down. Slowly, the silver filled up the river, burying the remains of the train and Latham Cole. Soon all that could be seen of Cole was his hand. It reached into the sky still clutching the pocket watch. And as they watched, that too was caught in the river, and disappeared from view.

Justice had been served.

CHAPTER 21

Promontory Summit was once again the site of a celebration. Though this time, they were not celebrating the meeting of two trains, but rather one man.

"Ladies and gentlemen," Habberman said to the gathered crowd. "We are here today to recognize something that has become far too rare. A genuine hero." He paused, nodding to Rebecca and Danny, who stood in the crowd. "As chairman of the Transcontinental Railroad, I'd like to express our gratitude to this masked man, this . . . Lone Ranger."

Walking onto the platform, the Lone Ranger approached Habberman.

"With a small token of our thanks," the big man said, holding out the same watch box he had offered

Cole not so long ago. "Time to take off the mask, son."

Looking out over the crowd, the Lone Ranger hesitated. If he took off the mask now, there would be no more Lone Ranger. And there was still justice to be served. His eyes locked with Rebecca's. He owed it to his brother's memory to keep the Lone Ranger name alive. Looking back at Habberman, he shook his head. "Not yet," he said.

Then he put his fingers between his lips and whistled. A moment later, the big white horse trotted up. Turning to Habberman, the Lone Ranger handed him back the box. The watch was gone. Inside was a handful of birdseed. With a tip of his hat, he hopped on his horse and rode over to Rebecca and Danny.

"Train's heading west," he said when he got to them. "Nothing holding you here anymore." He gazed down at Rebecca, nervous and hopeful about what she might say.

"It's my home," she said, her words echoing the ones he had said not too long before.

For a moment, neither of them said anything. Finally, the Lone Ranger nodded. He knew what Rebecca needed. "Man can't stay the same with the world evolving around him," he said, turning to look at Danny. "You're not a boy anymore. Your daddy would be proud. Look after your mama."

Danny nodded solemnly. He would do his best. And what he couldn't do, Rebecca could. Plus, the Lone Ranger thought, he was never going to be too far away. Saying good-bye, he galloped out of Colby, heading into the desert.

It didn't take the Lone Ranger long to find Tonto. The Comanche Indian was walking along, feeding his bird. Riding up to him, the Lone Ranger fell into step. "Thought I'd call him Silver," he said, petting his white horse. Then he threw his watch to Tonto.

"Good name," Tonto replied, trying the watch trick one more time. To his surprise, he got it! *Finally!*

Hiding a smile, the Lone Ranger nodded at the watch. "Just so you know, it's not actually a trade unless both parties agree." Tonto turned to him, eyebrow raised. "I mean, would you willingly trade a watch for birdseed?"

Tonto shrugged. "Bird can't tell time, Kemosabe."

The two friends continued on in silence for a while, each lost in his thoughts. Tonto could finally put his past behind him, while the Lone Ranger was uncertain of his future. But there was one thing the ranger wanted to get clear.

"Kemosabe?" he repeated. "You know, if we're going to be outlaws, I think I'm going to need a better name." He paused. "What about the Mask of Justice?"

"No," Tonto stated.

"The Lone Rider of—"

"No."

As the sun began to set on the horizon, the two men rode

on, bickering back and forth. Finally, the masked ranger had had enough. As he kicked his horse, the big animal reared up. "Hi-yo, Silver—away!" he cried before taking off, the horse's hooves kicking up a trail of dust. Behind him, Tonto patted his bird and then began to follow. Whatever happened next, it was going to be an interesting adventure.

EPILOGUE

It was time for the Wild West Show to close for the night. As the lights went off one by one, Will stood in front of the diorama, watching Tonto. The old man gazed out at the faux horizon, lost in thought.

"Guess I should be heading home," Will said, wishing he didn't have to.

"Home," Tonto repeated. His voice was filled with sadness and longing. Slowly, he raised his hat to his head, covering the stuffed bird.

"It was nice to meet you, Mr. Tonto," Will said, turning to go. Then he paused. Turning back, he eyed the Comanche. "So . . . the Windigo? Nature out of balance? The masked man? It's just a story, right?"

Tonto said nothing.

"I mean, I know he wasn't real . . . was he?"

Finally, Tonto spoke. "Up to you," he replied, tossing something to Will.

Will looked down. In his hand was a silver bullet.

Gasping, he raised his head, but Will was now alone. Tonto was gone. Slowly, Will reached up and lowered his mask over his eyes. "Never take off the mask," he said softly as he walked out of the Wild West Show and into the warm San Francisco night.